OUTCRY WITNESS
A NICOLE LONG LEGAL THRILLER

AIME AUSTIN

Outcry Witness

This edition published by
Moore Digital Media
1125 N Fairfax Blvd. #46071
Los Angeles CA 90046

Cover Designer: The Cover Collection
Outcry Witness/Aime Austin. — 2d ed.

eISBN: 978-1-64414-073-4
ISBN: 978-1-64414-108-3

THE NICOLE LONG LEGAL THRILLER SERIES

ALSO BY AIME AUSTIN

The Casey Cort Series of Legal Thrillers

But let justice roll down like waters, and righteousness like an ever-flowing stream.

—Amos 5:24

For all have sinned and fall short of the glory of God.

—ROMANS 3:23

ONE
NICOLE THERIOT LONG
JUNE 9, 1991

hadn't been in the front row of New Day in a very long time. J.T. Long, also known as my larger-than-life father was up on the stage preaching his heart out. He'd been plain old John Long up until he'd taken over the church during my last year of high school.

"So many of you have asked me how to survive this latest economic crisis," Daddy boomed. "I'm here to tell you there's no calamity. There's no disaster. The news anchors will fill your head with statistics, eight hundred thousand jobs lost, the Fed messing around with interest rates, a war that's come to an end with our boys swiftly victorious. Those are excuses. God does not like excuses."

I wanted to turn around, see how his message was landing with the three thousand people behind me. When I'd been up at Mt. Holyoke, a couple of my poli-sci professors had said blaming victims was a conservative political ploy to deflect culpability from where it truly lie, with those reckless enough to exploit deregulation, damned the consequences. The truth had to be somewhere in between, I figured.

The Amen chorus let me know they were good with it.

"But this I say: He who sows sparingly will also reap sparingly, and he who sows bountifully will also reap bountifully." Daddy paused for effect. "One gives freely, yet gains even more; another withholds what is right, only to become poor."

"Amen."

"A generous soul will prosper, and he who refreshes others will himself be refreshed. So before you blame God for not providing, look in your own field. Look in your own backyard. See if you've sowed enough seeds. See if you've given enough to others. Only when you've planted enough, given enough of yourself will you receive the bounty that is your due."

My father was a Catholic who was preaching like a Southern Baptist. New Day was officially non-denominational. He took donations from anyone who could give. Trust me, while he was telling people to not feel sorry for themselves, the other message was about donating freely.

The Proverbs were my Daddy's main vehicle for getting money in the church's coffers. While some of the congregation didn't weather the recession well, Momma, Daddy, and I were just fine. At the end of my college graduation ceremony a few weeks ago I'd gotten a diploma in my little leather case while lots of other girls had only an invoice.

After the choir closed the service, I tried my best to hustle to the back, but a grip on my arm stopped me. I turned to see Seth Collins was attached to that hand. He was my father's right hand and the associate pastor.

"Long time no see, Nicole. It's lovely that you've graced us with your presence here today."

June was hot in Baton Rouge, but I shivered nonetheless. Something about Collins had always felt off to me. More often than not, though, his wife was clinging to his side and our conversations were never more than perfunctory. I made an exaggerated move with my head, sweeping from right to left.

"Where's Rosalee?" His blond haired blue eyed wife was nowhere to be seen.

"Brandon brought home something from nursery. Got Crystal sick." Collins' head was bent close to mine.

"Ugh. Germs." I backed away, plucking his hand from my arm.

Finally Daddy broke away from the crowd of adoring churchgoers.

"Nicki Mouse," he started, his mouth bent to my ear. "Let's go back. There's something I want to talk about with you and Seth."

Before I could react, I did my best to school my face into something bland. I hadn't been raised as a preacher's kid, my father only having come into the game five years ago, but I'd learned that I should behave in church. My private life was still my own.

For as long as I could remember, my dad had been an executive at various oil and gas companies. When the industry turned upside down five years ago, he'd taken over New Day church. Since he'd never been religious, I saw it as just another hustle, albeit one without economic downturns.

His mammoth sized office was a carbon copy of the last one where he'd been a vice president. The only difference was an unabridged dictionary sized leather bound bible on his desk and a wall size wood plaque behind him with Romans 3:23 burned into it.

When my mother and Collins and I were in the room and Daddy's secretary had closed the door, everyone visibly relaxed. I was gratified to see that I wasn't the only one who tensed up under the constant scrutiny.

"Brought in a hundred and fifty three thousand this weekend. That's the estimate, at least. I'll get you the final numbers on Tuesday," Collins said.

I could feel my eyebrows rise involuntarily. Daddy would never say, but I had to wonder what his slice of the pie was. There was the new campus to support, but there were zero taxes on that.

"About thirty to fifty per person, then?" Mother said.

"You did that in your head?" Collins asked.

"Always been good with figures," Mother retorted. She'd never say it outright, but I think she didn't like Collins either. If we'd had a different kind of mother daughter relationship, maybe we'd have shared our opinions of the assistant pastor. I shook my head clear of the thoughts.

All this interpersonal stuff was kind of interesting, but I'd done my part, showing up as the dutiful daughter in my peach linen suit and floral blouse. I was ready to get back home to Metairie.

My parents hadn't moved to the New Day campus in Baton Rouge. Collins had the clergy house. Either I'd go to the club and swim or meet up with a friend for a late lunch. But I needed get out of here to get on with the rest of my day.

"What's up?" I directed my question at Daddy. He was the decision maker in the house *and* at New Day.

"You need a job." Mother's words were blunt.

Then daddy did what he always did, try to soften her words.

"It's not that we aren't glad to have you home, girl—"

"Here comes the 'but,'" I interrupted. I knew I sounded like the teenage years I just left. When my mother poked at me this way, I couldn't help myself.

"*But*...what are your *plans*?" Margaret Theriot Long's tone was serious, clipped. All that polite and syrupy Southern charm was not on display for me—her daughter —today. I'd only been home two weeks and the very conversation I'd hoped to avoid was already upon me.

I wish I'd taken some notes, prepped better. I was going into a knife fight, unarmed. A Southern woman did not come to a day like this unprepared. Four years up in Hadley, Massachusetts, had made me soft. I took a breath, conjured up the class discussion debating skills I'd honed over the time I'd been at an all-women's college. I had learned to spar with the best—smart women turned mean girls. My mother had nothing on those bitches.

"Mam, I graduated from college exactly three weeks ago. I'm trying to figure things out."

"Why didn't you figure things out before?" *Things* was

in air quotes. "I've already turned your room into my sewing room."

That was obvious. The dark purple walls were now pink, the color they'd been before I hit puberty, and decided that I wasn't made of sugar and spice and all things nice.

My double bed with its black and purple sugar skull comforter was gone, replaced by a frilly white eyelet coverlet over a very uncomfortable daybed. Two weeks trying to sleep on it and my back was starting to feel like that of a woman three times my age.

My posters of Wham! and Tears for Fears had gone missing. Probably up in the attic. *Hopefully* up in the attic. My mam thought they were all gay, and while gay could entertain, gay could not be idolized. It was the same with African-Americans. There was us, and there was all of *them*. I didn't agree. I never agreed, but that wasn't the fight I was going to fight today.

"Am I the unwelcome guest, then?" My voice was petulant once again. Unwanted wasn't a nice feeling. "Three days and I'm out like the fish from Friday's dinner?"

"Kiki, come on. It's not that. Your dad and I are thrilled to have you visit..."

Even behind the nickname, my mother's term of endearment for me for as long as I could remember, I heard her meaning. I was a visitor. I was a guest. I'd stink after too many days, and it had already been fourteen. I didn't point out those facts. Instead, I tried others.

"There's research out now that says that at least

thirty-six percent of adult children live with their parents," I argued. "My being here is not an anomaly."

"That means sixty-four percent are out on their own." That last bit of math had come from my father whose voice boomed as he stepped from behind the seven foot expanse of wood that made up his desk.

In a moment, his hand was on the lid of our family's cookie jar, lifting and poking through the contents. Our girl...woman, Aubrey Theriot—no relation—always kept that stocked with his favorite pecan Sandies. For a moment I wondered who was in charge of getting the homemade treats from Metairie to Baton Rouge.

"Your *sister* didn't move back home," Mother added.

Despite the fact that Michelle was married with two kids and living in Dallas, they'd kept *her* room intact. All frilly lace on her huge canopy bed and horse posters hadn't been so much as touched since she'd moved out. No one had suggested I sleep in there.

My sister had always been my mother's favorite, a fact I'd never called her on because I'd always been afraid she'd admit the truth of it.

Thinking something was one thing. Knowing it for sure could be devastating. Either way, I didn't know what Michelle's marriage to some rich Texas oil guy had to do with my need to have some time to figure out my next steps, nor why we were having the conversation here in front of Seth Collins. My desperation at not being tossed out on my ear overcame my need for privacy.

"Daddy, it's harder out there now than it was for your generation," I argued. "Student loans, a weak economy, stagnant wages...that haven't increased in twenty years."

"I know what the word stagnant means. Do you have loans I don't know about?" my dad asked around a mouthful of flour, sugar, and nuts. "Last time I checked, I wrote the tuition checks to that school in the back of beyond Massachusetts."

"No, Daddy, I don't have loans. You know that." He'd deflated me without even swallowing his snack. "I was just saying there are a lot of reasons kids come home."

"Maybe one day I'll debate with you about that thirty-six percent you cite. Could be an interesting sociological discussion. But I don't have to parent or feed any of those arrested adults, except through the high taxes I pay. So tell me, Nicky Mouse, what's your plan?"

My dad's use of his nickname for me calmed me a little. I was still *his* favorite. He still loved me, only it was a form of tough love that I wasn't enjoying at the moment.

"I don't know, yet. I thought I'd take the summer—"

"When you went to that school, you said it would be a great place to meet contacts. The only contacts you seemed to have made are lots of dykes."

"James Long, that's not a word we can use anymore," my mother admonished, her pointer finger wagging. Then her voice lowered to a whisper. "Like Negro."

I turned to see that Seth Collins hadn't flinched at the impropriety. Whether 1991 Louisiana was the new south or the old south, it was like a mine field sometimes figuring what people's true thoughts or intentions were.

"Fine. Girls who like girls. It was like they were there

to study other women. If you'd gone to Duke or even Tulane, you'd be in a different position. You'd have certainly met the right people. Could have joined Alpha Delta Phi like your mother."

"Dad. How many times did I have to tell you I didn't want to major in business or marketing and get some soul-sucking job that would do nothing to help women or men or the greater good."

"I'm sorry, I must have blinked. Do you have one of those jobs now? A do-gooder job at a charity?" Before he could clutch his heart Red Foxx-style, I cut in.

"Well...no."

I felt like a bear lumbering into some kind of trap, but I was unable to pivot fast enough to avoid whatever he had planned for me.

An internship at a dysfunctional nonprofit had cured me of that dream. Without the future mapped out just so, my mind was wiped clean at the thought of a career. It was all a blank canvas and I didn't have any paint.

"Religion major of all the damned things." My father shook his head like he had every time he'd repeated this refrain. He knew I wasn't a believer. I'd never explained that it felt like a case of know your enemy. "You know what? The church is a business too. That can actually help people. Why don't you get a job here?"

Seth Collins' presence kept me from expressing my true feelings about daddy's proposal.

"What would I do?" I threw up my hands. "Religious studies at Mount Holyoke isn't like a seminary program.

I'm not qualified to do anything here. At *this* place." I could feel my eyebrows crawling up my forehead.

Most people tried to talk themselves into a job. I was trying to talk myself out.

"You say it like 'brothel,' Nicky Mouse. It's a multimillion-dollar business not much different from oil."

Oil had his business. It's what had paid for the country club I was itching to get to, my fancy private high school, and Seven Sister college education. The origin of our wealth was a fact I kept to myself while I was in Hadley. Especially with the campus protests after the Exxon Valdez spill. I didn't share anything about this second career either. There weren't two things more polarizing than fossil fuels and religion.

"Is New Day approaching megachurch status now with an entire staff to push religion out to the masses?" I asked in my debate voice. "During brunch a few months back, I think I saw something in the *New York Times* about the growth of American religiosity and fundamentalism."

If my dad had been at home, he'd have arranged his face into a sneer of derision. He was a Southerner of a different type, a Texan. My mother had softened some of his edges over the years they'd been married.

"You're standing right here, free to leave. It's a church, not a cult," he retorted. "These damn Yankees occasionally come down to the 'Cotton States' to see what the other half of the country is up to, so it's possible they wrote something about New Day."

My mother flashed me a look and I knew that we were going to leave the 'Cotton States' comment alone. I looked around the room again, but Collins' face was a bland as tapioca pudding.

"What do you think I could actually do here?"

"You haven't really figured out what area you'd like to focus on. I still maintain you can't go wrong with marketing and public relations. I don't know all the right words, I'll let Seth tell it. It was his brilliant idea."

Boom went the dynamite. Snap went the trap. I was like those pigs and cows who were blindly corralled into a slaughter house. This had been the plan all along. My hindsight was a perfect twenty-twenty.

"Hey, I know that you probably have plans for the rest of the day. Why don't we get together first thing Monday morning," Collins offered. "Bring a resume and we'll talk."

Mam and Daddy had always said that I couldn't live with them past eighteen without a job. Or a husband to take care of me. Now I knew they'd been dead serious. I was guessing that whatever Seth offered, declining it wouldn't be an option.

TWO
NICOLE
JUNE 12, 1991

Contrary to how I'd spun it for my parents, I'd no more than skimmed the megachurch article in the *New York Times*. I'd been born and raised in the South. Though I'd never agree with my father out loud, northern newspaper articles about Louisiana and the rest of the states below the Mason-Dixon line had a bit of a "zoo" observational aspect that turned my stomach queasy. As if our lives were nothing more than bonus scenes from *Deliverance*.

Once I'd navigated to the address I had scribbled on a Post-it affixed to the dashboard, I have to admit I was surprised. New Day was not my grandmother's church. It had been a couple of years at least since I'd come here. Last Sunday, I'd paid no attention on the drive from home to the sanctuary's auditorium where daddy was preaching.

I'd been too busy spending the hourlong drive trying to navigate the minefield that was conversation with my mother. Aubrey's husband, Fabian had pulled up the tinted windowed Lincoln to a back door and Mother and I had entered and taken our seats only moments before the service began.

What daddy was creating was an entirely new breed of house of worship. I followed half a dozen signs that put me into some kind of visitor parking. I stepped out of the car into the muggy heat.

June had never been anything but hot and humid in Louisiana. Spending the last few summers up north in Boston and New York had made me soft. I sucked in as much of the humid air as I could and took in my surroundings. The place where daddy had preached was high up on a hill. I was now on flat ground.

The building in front of me was modern and huge. I spun around on my wedge-heeled sandals and took in the campus. Up until this moment, I'd only associated that word with schools, but it was exactly what this was. It had to be at least half the eight hundred acres of my college grounds in the western Massachusetts' wilderness.

Brand-new brick buildings dotted the subtropical landscape. The signs I'd seen after I'd gotten on the campus had various ministries and arrows—children went one way, women another, and students yet another. I'd been driving too fast to read the rest.

The engraved eight-foot-wide concrete sign at this, the main office building entrance, had a painted dove next to the church's name. I locked my car, then followed the path to the front door. The air-conditioning inside hit me like a blast from a freezer.

When I was a kid, A/C hadn't yet been a thing and I'd sweltered through more school days and church mornings than I'd like to count. But this new temperature-controlled South required I carry a cardigan everywhere. I took a few steps back to my car and pulled the forgotten blue sweater from the passenger seat.

When I walked in the second time, sweater securely buttoned at my neck, I tried not to gawp like a tourist at the soaring ceilings and preternatural silence. Over the last couple of years, Daddy had said something about building and renovations, but I'd never paid much attention.

My experience with church was a small gothic Catholic parish with a couple of old nuns, an older priest, lots of incense, and even more Latin. This was like a Southern college campus. I craned my head wondering if there was a cafeteria. A bunch of fresh-faced students would not have been out of place.

My hip checked something hard. Snapped out of my wonder, I realized I'd literally run into the reception desk. As I massaged my sore flesh, I took in the polished woman at the desk. If there was a single thing I missed while up at school, it was a woman who pulled herself together.

Somehow being at a women's college meant that half the students didn't bother to wear real pants much less comb their hair. Plaid pajamas bottoms and bedhead weren't uncommon in morning classes. The afternoon upgrade had been sweats and a ponytail.

Then at dinner, these same women would wonder why they didn't have boyfriends. In the beginning, I'd point out it could be because of their choice of a women's college and their slovenly appearance. Not one person had taken my comments or advice to heart.

I'd had no problem attracting the interest of men at UMass or even Amherst. Makeup and a skirt went far. When I'd given up answering that same question time and again, my housemates had blinked at my impolite silence in the face of their perplexity.

"Good morning," the well-coiffed woman said. "Welcome to New Day. How can I help you?"

"Nicole Long. I have an eight o'clock appointment with Seth Collins."

The woman bowed her head and scanned a large day planner, her pencil ticking through the fifteen-minute-increment boxes.

"Yes. Here you are, penciled in by Pastor Collins himself." I could hear the reproof in her voice. Seth Collins had probably gone off script at my father's behest. "Please have a seat, and I'll let the *pastor* know you're here."

I was about to scope out the seating situation when a loud booming voice stopped me in my tracks.

"Nicole Long. You have your mother's eyes."

"My mother?" I asked.

At my question, his eyes went the tiniest bit wide for a second.

"Yes, your mother. Blue as the Texas sky."

I let the comment slide. My mother's eyes were hazel. I had Daddy's eyes.

"Texas?" I asked eschewing formality.

"Houston born and raised," Collins said while beating his left hand against his heart.

Now I knew that geography was what the associate pastor and my father had as common ground because my father was more sinner than saint, despite this reinvention of himself as pious church leader.

Eventually, I took his extended hand in mine and gave it a firm shake.

"Let's talk in my office," he said. Collins gestured toward a nearly invisible door, the handle the only protuberance in the blond wood expanse.

The office was nearly as big and as spacious as my daddy's, practically shouting Pastor Collins' importance as my dad's right hand man. Daddy hadn't said so, but my guess was that Collins did the day to day business of running the church while my father was gladhanding. Finding investors for his oil business had never been a problem. Probably even easier to raise money in the name of God.

I looked around Collins' office as I waited for him to take his place in whatever he considered the seat of power.

There was a seating area on one side with a love seat and two upholstered chairs. A small conference area with a table that seated six, then a desk that was anything but modest, and floor-to-ceiling bookshelves rounded out the furniture collection.

Propriety required that I wait until I was invited to sit. Since this was a favor to my father, my main goal was to do the minimum necessary to make sure I had a place to sleep while I looked for my next real move, and not piss anyone off.

I wanted Pastor Collins to tell my father I'd made a lovely impression but wasn't experienced enough to get a pass on the obvious nepotism play. No harm, no foul. I inched toward the chairs opposite the desk ready to lay my portfolio on one seat and my bum on another for the brief, obligatory interview.

"Let's not be formal," Collins boomed into the silence. Now that my father wasn't taking up all the air in the room, I could see one reason why daddy had chosen Collins.

He had one of those Southern preacher voices. "For some reason, churches make people whisper. Fifteen years ago, when I wasn't much older than you, my uncle founded New Day because he wanted worship to be something real. Something that wasn't all rarified air. If we want to bring people to God, we shouldn't make it so damned hard."

I was trying to take in all the information. Daddy had mentioned taking over a church. It had been so out of character in some ways, that I hadn't asked who'd been running it before. My excuse that nepotism would be the cause of impropriety was starting to look like it might not fly.

During his little speech, Collins was walking and gesturing toward the small seating area. This time I did lay down my portfolio on an upholstered chair before I smoothed my skirt and took a spot on the narrow leather couch. Collins took the other chair but not before scooting it closer to me.

I unbuttoned the sweater at my neck. It was warmer in here than in the lobby.

"I forget how hot it can be in Louisiana."

"I'm surprised it bothered you," he said.

I was about to interject about how the air conditioning made it hard to calibrate temperature when he spoke.

"It's hot in Africa."

For a moment, I was quiet. Did he have me confused with someone else? A girl with a blue-eyed mom who'd volunteered for the Peace Corps? Had my dad mentioned our relationship on Sunday? I thought it was obvious from his admonition that I get a job, but maybe not. Maybe my mother's coldness had called any family relationship into question. Wouldn't be the first time.

I decided to go with quiet rather than call Collins out on the possibly embarrassing mistake. He'd figure it out soon enough all on his own.

"So, what are you looking for?" His guileless open face was oddly welcoming. I wanted to lean closer. Give him a good answer. I didn't have one, though, because I was a bit taken aback by the question. I was mostly expecting something more perfunctory like asking me about my college experience or major or where I saw myself in five years. Or even about my dad's golf game, my mother's volunteer activities. Those questions I'd asked and answered myself on the long drive over.

"I...uh...I just graduated and am looking to find my footing in the working world," came out of my mouth haltingly. It wasn't actually saying anything at all, but it was me speaking and not looking as clueless as I felt.

Collins placed a hand on mine, which had been holding my knee down to stop it from bobbing nervously. A shiver went through me. I didn't think it was attraction, but I couldn't place the feeling. Before I had any time to parse it, he was speaking. He'd lowered booming to amiable.

"Your diction is perfect, by the way. You'll be fine."

"Um, thank you," I said with hesitation in my voice. He had to know that I'd only gone to top schools. Did he think that there was something wrong with me that I was unemployed after graduation? Maybe there was something to what momma and daddy were saying. If I hadn't gotten my MRS degree, then I needed to kickstart my career. The work world was ruthless.

Collins didn't move his hand. Just squeezed as if he'd made a decision, then he spoke again.

"Let me tell you what I have available, then you can tell me what you think. Your father did say that you were a bit at loose ends, but that you'd been thinking about something on the softer side of things—journalism, public relations, or the like."

I found my head nodding. That sounded like the kind of picture Daddy would have painted before he'd ambushed me. No matter that it wasn't dead-on accurate. My options, though, were looking like they weren't many. So much for the 1990s rallying cry of women being able to do anything they wanted.

"I thought a girl like you with a fine education would

be a great fit for New Day," Collins continued. "We're looking for a new public relations assistant to join our director. Things are changing. This isn't your grandmother's church outreach. No typed bulletins with cake recipes are enough to keep them engaged. Nor is the word of the Lord sufficient anymore. These days people want to know what a church can do for them."

"Are you saying you want me to sell the people...God?" I could feel my hair swish around my face as my head shook. What he was saying didn't jibe at all with my experience. The Catholic church I'd grown up in was a take it or leave it kind of institution. These non-denominational mega churches were a different breed, I guessed

"Sell them God. Sell them church. Sell them redemption. Sell them salvation. Take your pick."

"That feels cynical." The words were out before I could help myself.

"The Bible says in the gospel according to Mark, 'Go into all the world and preach the gospel to every creature. He who believes and is baptized will be saved; but he who does not believe will be condemned.' I know that the Pope and *your* faith have a lot of rules. At the same time, they're hemorrhaging the faithful like blood from a gunshot wound."

I couldn't help but nod in agreement. Even in *Ireland* the church was losing parishioners.

"New Day wants to save souls, not lose them," Collins continued. His voice was warm and syrupy sweet like honey. "I may not be a cynic, but you'll find out that I'm a realist. We're competing with five hundred television channels, movies, video games, alcohol, sex, and sin. It takes savvy public relations to push back against that."

I may not agree with everything he'd said, but he had a point. Catholics in both Louisiana and Texas were still reeling from the Gilbert Gauthe sex abuse scandal. And the Gauthe crimes felt like the tip of the iceberg.

I was more interested in the job now than I'd been in the twelve hours before. The other reason my father had probably recommended me for this job was that my major had been in religion.

I'd never had any particular interest in the subject when I was younger. In fact, I'd stopped going to church after my confirmation, and my father's latest venture surely wasn't the reason. But one good professor had piqued my interest during a sophomore year survey class and I was hooked. Religion, more than almost anything else, was the driving force behind much of human behavior.

THREE
NICOLE
JUNE 12, 1991

"What would I do?" I asked intrigued.

"In the book of Revelation heaven is people from every tribe and every language and every nation. You have the perfect background for increasing our diversity. Churches in the south have been segregated for far too long."

I nodded. A well-timed 'amen' wouldn't have been amiss, but the call and response of his kind of church was as foreign to me as Latin and incense would be to him.

Collins continued, "You'll need to work with our team to find effective ways to reach new congregants. Work to keep the current ones engaged in what we do here. You'd have a lot of autonomy on how you'd decide to do that. I'm not saying that Jesus is for everyone. What I'm saying is that a smart young woman like yourself could really cut her teeth. Then, when you're ready, you can go to New York or Boston."

"Why do you think I'd leave?" I asked, though I knew deep down in my bones that I would.

"Women like you? They always leave. You come back thinking that Louisiana, the South will be your home again. But once you move north, you're changed. This place will eventually chafe. When that day comes, we'll give you a party and send you on your way. What I'm saying, though, is that this job will teach you a lot and put you on the path to wherever you want to go."

My mother had always said if something seemed too good to be true...

"Why are you doing this? Surely you must have a long list of applicants."

"The position hasn't been advertised, so no list. When your dad shared how lost you were, I wanted to help. Ministering to those in need is the actual definition of my job."

I started to protest.

"I'm not—" Collins swiftly interrupted.

"Preaching the word of God is not the only way to minister people. Something about your name or your story or the picture of you in your cap and gown that your dad shared called to me. It was as if God whispered in my ear that I would be called upon to help you in any way I could.

"In a state like Louisiana, I don't spend any time trying to talk people out of blindly following the Pope and going to Mass. But what I can do is help you. Give you the space and time to figure out what you want all the while helping you to learn lifelong skills."

"What do you get out of it?"

"One very loyal employee."

"Loyal?"

"The position starts at seventy-two thousand."

It was only a nanosecond lapse before I caught myself, but I knew my jaw had nearly dropped open in shock. Loyalty? With money like that, he could buy a lot more than loyalty.

"If you need time to think it over, the offer stands until Friday close of business. After that, I'll move on to the next step."

"I'll take it." I spoke well before I could form a thought or make a thorough analysis of the pros and cons of putting a Southern megachurch on my résumé—my soon-to-be northern city calling card.

"I'd hoped that's what you would say. Let's formally put your start date at..." He gazed at a Palm Pilot that seemed to materialize out of nowhere. "The seventeenth of June."

I nodded my acceptance. Thought about what I'd do with my last five days of freedom. Tried not to spend the six thousand a month that would be mine without strings.

"Good. I'll walk you over to payroll. Gosh now, it's all Human Resources. I'll take you over there to get the paperwork set up. First lesson, don't spend your whole paycheck on new sneakers, okay?"

I looked down at my modest heels, then toward his very shiny loafers and did an internal shrug. Maybe that's what he thought my generation wore to work nowadays. I silently vowed to myself to drive over to

Macy's at the Lakeside and add more pumps to my wardrobe.

"Why don't you come to my office when you arrive? I'll introduce you to your new boss, Lana Hawkins, then she and I can lay out the New Day vision for you."

"All that works." I stood and gathered my portfolio. He'd never even asked to see the résumé I'd rushed to get printed on heavy cream stock.

Finally, he stood and we walked toward the door. Then, offhandedly, he said, "Oh, you'll be coming from Metairie every day, right? How was that drive this morning?"

Even with a throwaway question, Collins' face was creased in genuine interest. He was an odd duck. Maybe he actually did care? Though if pressed, I'd still say it was all an act. I left open the possibility that I may be judged him too hastily and answered the question asked.

"Not too bad. About an hour, but traffic was okay this early. I figured maybe I'd catch a ride with my father some days..." I stopped speaking because announcing your daddy would drive you to work was not the height of professionalism. Nepotism was one thing, immaturity another.

"I do have another suggestion," Collins offered.

"Go ahead."

"It's up to you, but we do have a small apartment building on the grounds you could use. Nothing fancy, but we have a couple of studios available. Furnished. If that's something you think would make your commute easier. Happy to oblige."

I was both surprised and not that there was housing here on a church campus. Even from my quick glance around while driving, it was pretty obvious that New Day certainly had everything else.

"I'll think about it," I said. On the one hand, it would solve the problem of my home situation. On the other hand, something in my gut was rebelling. I wanted to take a minute to listen to the voice in my head. Collins gripped my shoulder with his hand, but not before sweeping my hair back. I almost flinched but caught myself.

Southern men were more touchy-feely than anyone I'd encountered in the northeast. Maybe Collins was right and I was changed. I didn't want to be, so I employed the skills of a polite southern woman and laid my hand on the arm outstretched toward me so he didn't get any closer.

"That one also comes with an expiration date," Collins said with a shoulder squeeze to emphasize his point. "There's a list of folks that would be interested in the living space if it's not up to your liking."

I flashed on the last two weeks I'd been home. My sleeping accommodations had alternated between the couch in my father's study or the daybed in my mother's.

The latter was more comfortable, but I had to lift piles of yarn and bolts of fabric each night. It was like there were fairies in the house in reverse because every night, I found everything had materialized back on the daybed like I'd never moved them. It was my mother at her passive-aggressive best. I may have been able to eventually outwit her and her backward fairies, but Collins' generous offer gave me a handy solution to a problem I hadn't even planned on solving right away.

"You'll have a lot in common with your neighbors. About half are from East Baton Rouge," Collins added.

For a long second, I wondered about commonalities. East Baton Rouge was known as a diverse area, about half black and half white. Maybe it had a lot of college graduates or people in the middle of transition or God forbid he meant lesbians.

I didn't seek clarification, because I probably wasn't going to like the answer. Everyone down here thought I'd gone to an all-women's college because I liked women. It was a narrow-minded path I didn't wish to traverse before I'd even started the job. I guessed I'd learn a lot about the area and the church's values once I started the job.

"I'll take it." I'd made the split-second decision when I started thinking about whether I'd be able to open the windows of my father's study wide enough to get the smoke out tonight. After the drive back, I wouldn't be up to heavy lifting.

"Let me take you over," Collins said. He backed away from me, then shrugged off his sport coat, rolled up his sleeves as he prepared for the heat. "Show you the place first just to be sure."

On the way over, Collins filled me in on the history of the church, the evolution of all the ministries, and the Bentley his congregation had splurged on for him last Christmas. I managed to control my eyebrows on that last one. My father was still driving his usual Cadillac. He had a new one every year. I hadn't thought about who may be funding it.

The small apartment building was obviously new, the bricks still clay colored, not a whisp of ivy or other vines anywhere near the mortar.

"Oh, this is nice." Swiftly I put the cardigan I was carrying up to my mouth. I hadn't meant to say any of that out loud.

Seth Collins' laugh was a bark of surprise.

"It's okay. You're not the first. For some reason people hear 'church' and they think 'public housing.'" Collins, ever the gentleman, put his hand at the small of my back. I hoped he didn't feel the damp sweat gathering there.

"Here, let me get the door for you," he offered, then stepped aside to pull it open.

The door was plate glass. Not a single smudge marred the pristine surface. The upper part of the building was covered in siding that reminded me of Cape Cod with its blue-gray color. We took a silently swift stainless-steel elevator to the fifth floor. At five oh three, Collins produced a key from his pocket. Opened the door. Following his prompt, I stepped in front of him and walked through the door.

It was gorgeous. There was no other word for it. Modern, too. Nothing like I was used to in New Orleans or anywhere in Louisiana. The walls were bright but not a harsh white. A compact but fully equipped kitchen was on the left. A small bathroom on the right.

A huge walk-in closet was just beyond that. It wasn't much bigger than my senior dorm room, but there was enough space in the well-laid-out plan for a double bed, breakfast table and chairs, full-size sofa and coffee table. A huge Trinitron was on a console opposite the couch.

"They all have cable TV and air. Not sure we get BET or anything like that, but MTV for sure."

I decided to forego the bait he dangled. I was not in the mood to defend the taste of today's youth. I only hoped I could shut that down once I started working and they realized that twenty-somethings weren't all frivolous music video junkies. I had seventy-two thousands reasons to make a good impression.

"Who is all this for?" I asked. My arms spread out to encompass all that I was seeing.

This was not your average church shelter. Priests and nuns didn't have it this good. Not that evangelicals or any Christians took a vow of poverty. The Bentley was evidence of that.

"It's for whomever needs it. During one of our first congregation surveys, we found there was a huge need for transitional housing. Divorce. Short-term unemployment. As I'm sure you learned at that fancy school of yours, our country doesn't have much of a safety net. Churches have long been that. New Day aims to be that, too, but in the modern century."

"So how does this work?" I was already peeling some bills off my paycheck to pay for this. I'd consider it my donation to the church.

Collins walked to the kitchen counter and picked up a set of keys. He lifted my hand. I opened it reflexively, my sweater falling to the ground. He ignored that and instead placed the keys gently into my palm, then closed my fingers around them.

The air crackled with something, but I couldn't pinpoint it. My stomach felt a bit odd again, but I ignored that and instead bent as gracefully as I could in a pencil skirt and retrieved my fallen garment from the shiny wood floors. The grain caught my attention, and I realized it was repeated. The wood looked good but wasn't real.

"The keys are yours. There on the fridge are the numbers of anyone I think you'll need. Facilities. Maintenance. Off-hours emergency."

I glanced at the printed magnet. Everything was slick. No scarred floors. No frayed edges. No wrinkled paper.

"Thank you. This is just what I needed," I admitted.

Collins' hand came out, smoothed down my hair, then snatched his hand back as if he were surprised by something. The gesture was both intimate and not, paternal, but not quite.

Without comment, he stepped back out of my space.

"Parking's in back. The spaces are numbered by apartment. I'll see you Monday, then?"

"What time do you start?"

"Nine on the dot. People get the South all wrong. We're very civilized."

FOUR
NICOLE
OCTOBER 31, 1991

"Y ou're late," Lana Hawkins barked before I could slip the purse from my shoulder and jam it into the desk drawer.

The clock in the lobby had read 9:05 when I walked in. I was the only person in this building who was busted for time. It had to be the perils of this being my just out of college job.

Everyone acted as if I had no skills because I was twenty-two. Or maybe they were riding me hard because of my dad. In three and a half months, I'd worked hard to prove them wrong on both counts. From Hawkins' tone, it was clear all that labor wasn't getting me very far.

"I was just out in the Redemption lot checking on the decorations."

"This better work, because you're repurposing the biggest lot on a Thursday. That's our biggest bible study night."

"It's Halloween, Lana. We'll double the number of people who would come on any Thursday because they'll bring their kids. Plus I looked at attendance numbers for past years and Halloween is like a ghost town. Pun intended."

Hawkins did not crack a smile.

"Some of the board members have called wondering how in the heck we've started dealing in the profane." Hawkins added to the list of grievances. I really hadn't talked to daddy about any of this, but maybe it was time to have him weigh in on the over involved elder members.

I was never so grateful to see my extension ringing. Some volunteers wanted me back outside to get more info about set up. Everything about Hawkins matched with the hallmarks of a good boss. Something about her rubbed me the wrong way. Instead of a mentor relationship, it was more of a boss employee one. Not that it was bad exactly, just not as friendly. Collins constantly talked about how New Day was one big family. Hawkins was like a mean older sister. I already had one of those, I didn't need another.

A full twelve hours later, I was at my computer, exhausted, but triumphant. I'd had a couple of the security guards hold counters in their hands, and at least half the congregation had come to New Day's inaugural trunk or treat. That was more than we'd had at most Sunday sermons. Attendance had been far more in line with Easter or Christmas numbers.

"It's late."

I jumped at the voice. I'd thought I was in the office all alone. Church did not inspire the same dedication as finance or business. Most everyone was out at five o'clock on the dot.

"Did you not finish your sermon?" I asked. It was the only reason Collins ever stayed late. Daddy had been allowing Collins to preach one or two Sundays a month. The associate pastor walked the talk of time with family. He was home—across campus—for dinner every night except Sunday. On Sunday his picture perfect wife and kids sat at a head table in the banquet room where a weekly potluck kept people at New Day for a few more hours.

"Just typed the last few words."

"What are you going to talk about?" I asked with genuine interest.

Collins was good at building not only a sermon, but a theme. In September he'd talked about work and dedication, jumping off from Labor Day. This month he'd talked about family. I didn't see it at first, but he'd really fired up people to do more for each other. I'd worked with him hand in hand to grow before and after school care and our own bus service.

I'd worked on just the right wording and graphics on the flyers we'd handed out that first Sunday. In three weeks, we'd doubled enrollment in our kids' programs. Now the families were here nearly every weekday dropping their kids off or picking them up. Like a village, Collins had boomed from the pulpit. Families were interacting with each other, the kids as well. I might not believe in God, but I was starting to believe in Seth Collins.

"Are you going home?" Collins pointed at the glowing monitor in front of me.

"I was just putting together a memo on attendance, donations, and costs."

"That can wait. Walk with me. I'd love to hear how things went today. It was a very innovative idea."

If there was a single thing I knew could make my path at New Day smoother, it was facetime with the boss.

"Can it wait ten minutes? I wanted to get this to Lana first thing in the morning." Collins was Hawkins' boss. Except for daddy, he was everyone's boss. But that didn't mean he could get me off the hook for this assignment. Hawkins was a hell of a taskmaster.

"I'd like to talk to you about how you can grow your role here."

I didn't say no twice. Instead I grabbed for the cardigan I kept on the back of my chair. Collins took it from me and held it up. I slipped my right arm through one sleeve, and when he pivoted, my other arm through the left.

"Thank you," I demurred as I tried to figure out how to move farther away from him. Collins always walked that line between friendly and inappropriate. He'd never crossed it, but I didn't want to be the woman who made him sin.

I made a show of squatting as well as I could in my cotton dress and extracting my purse from the drawer.

Collins took the hint and pulled the office door open in anticipation of our exit.

"Glad you're spending your money wisely," he said as we crossed from the main office building to the first of the series of paved paths that led to the residential building.

I shrugged, then pulled the sweater closed as it nearly slipped from one of my shoulders. All my jerky movements made me trip as the tip of my mules caught in a sidewalk seam and I had to grab onto Collins for support.

"Sorry. All thumbs today."

"Every human body has a limit," he offered in absolution. "You really worked it out there today. The kids loved it. The parents loved it.

"What about the board? Lana told me there was some pushback on New Day having its hand in a profane holiday."

"Ah, the book of Timothy and apostasy."

I nodded as if I knew what in the hell he was talking about. I'd just been trying to make small talk, and Lana Hawkins' last complaint had been at the forefront of my mind. Ultimately, she'd let me organize the trunk or treat. No doubt the success would speak volumes against any objections.

"Throughout human history, Christmas was at the crossroads of secular and profane. It's the best rebranding ever in human history. A marketer like you could learn something from that."

"That's true," I said. "It was one of the most surprising things I think I learned in college. It went from a small winter solstice holiday on a pagan calendar to the second most sacred celebrating the birth of Jesus Christ."

"Bing! Bing! Bing! You're right on target. Halloween is no different. It was another end of the season—this time summer—festival. Pitched up alongside All Saints Day, it's another winner. You should know tt wasn't your dad, *I'm* the one that went to the mat for you on your trunk or treat idea."

"Thank you." I'd wondered how Hawkins had reversed course so quickly.

"I'm your guardian angel here to protect you."

When we got to my building, I paused before unlocking the front door.

"Thanks again for going to bat for me. I know that secular celebrations aren't exactly in New Day's wheel-house, but you did say to use my creativity to brainstorm new ways to get members of varying traditions more involved."

"You're a smart cookie." His hand that was probably aiming to pat my cheek, slipped and hit my boob instead. "Gotta take advantage of that."

I waved my own hands about impotently.

"It's been a long day. I'm going to hit the hay pretty early."

Collins looked at his watch, then used his own set of keys to unlock and pull the door open wide. I didn't have much choice but to accept his chivalry and walk through it and into the small lobby.

From habit I pulled out my tiny mailbox key to see what was in there. The empty metal box mocked me.

"Did you have problems with mail forwarding?"

I shook my head as I locked the rectangular door.

"Other than bills, I don't get much here. My parent's house is still my permanent address," I said while I walked to the elevator. He beat me to the lift and had pressed the call button before I could.

When the bell pinged and the door opened, I didn't have the words to suggest the lobby be his last stop. Going to a women's college hadn't prepared me for moments like this. At school, I'd just tip my head and point out it was a brick building full of women and most guys would nod and back away in a mild panic at that much estrogen coming their way.

Once at my floor, Collins waited for me to get out. For a long second, I sincerely hoped that he would stay in, press 'G' and get back to writing sermons or soothing members or even going home to his wife and kids. None of that happened right then. Instead he was out of the car as the heavy metal doors whooshed together with a silent snick.

"I know you're tired. Won't keep you. But I'd love to have a peek inside to see what you've done with the place, if you don't mind. All the girls here do something a little different."

He hadn't asked anything inappropriate, so I couldn't think of an objection to raise. Collins fiddled with his keys, and I wondered if he kept pass keys on his chain. As I found my own door key, I shook my head. No one would keep pass keys unless they were a janitor. The key to the front door was different I guess.

I could see him needing access to any building on a moment's notice. Tenant personal space was a different matter altogether, of course.

After I twisted the key in the lock, and pushed the door open, I stepped in tentatively. He bustled in behind me, his wide palm flat on the door, pushing it wide. He was a tad too close. I quickened my steps and walked in further than I'd planned in order to get away from the weird combination of heat and goosebumps the proximity of his front to my back caused.

"Looks almost lived in," he said while taking in the little touches I'd added to make the space my own.

"Used to dorm life, I guess," I responded. "Don't want to change anything so drastically that the next woman who needs it can't move right in and make it her own."

The use of 'woman' on my part was deliberate. I'd wondered what Collins was implying when he'd discussed me having much in common with the other tenants. Not much, was what I'd have answered to anyone who'd asked. It appeared that most of them were young black women who were down on their luck. Guy in jail. No family to fall back upon. Grateful to the church.

The only thing I shared with them was gender. Given my salary compared to what any of them appeared to be earning, I should probably have gone out and gotten my own place. But the savings of five or six hundred dollars a month would go a long way to a rental deposit when I finally made the move to New York or Boston or even Los Angeles. I wasn't doing anything to punch this gift horse in the mouth.

The closet was an open affair and Collins got a little too familiar with my clothes flicking through the hangers with the skill of someone stocking clothes at the Gap. I couldn't think of an objection to that either. He'd seen me in most of the clothes. What could be wrong with him seeing the clothes themselves devoid of a human form?

FIVE
NICOLE
OCTOBER 31, 1991

"Glad you're not one of those Hillni— Hilfiger types to spend all of their money on something as trivial as flash in the pan fashion."

"Saving up for the future," I said. "The money *is* excellent." I was making more than a fellow alum who was at Goldman Sachs, and she was working eighty hours a week and not-so-secretly sleeping under her desk.

"Is that SoCo?" Collins pointed to a small leather tray with matching cut glass decanter and glasses and a bottle of Southern Comfort.

"It was a gag gift," I deflected.

"Aren't you going to offer your guest something?" He used his hands to gesture toward himself sweeping up and down his clothing.

"Right," I sprang into action. My manners. "Would you like water. Tea?"

"Join me in a drink."

"Oh, okay," I said. I twisted open the bottle, breaking the seal. I poured one finger for him and a little less for myself.

"Don't be shy. I may be your boss, but I know you have a life outside of work."

I added a bit more to my glass so it more closely resembled his.

"Today we had six hundred seventy kids come through. Families volunteered seventy-seven cars," I reported as if this were no different than any post event rundown in the office.

"What were collections?"

"From the trunkers, we got seventy-seven hundred. Twenty-three hundred from the families."

"Ten thousand dollars total, then?"

"Yup. Plus we have some great publicity photos. The trunkers were happy to donate, help out the other families, and their kids got to decorate and hand out candy to the less fortunate. The other families got to bring their kids somewhere where they were welcome. The Brookstown families were happy to pay about twenty dollars per family to avoid the looks from the folks in Longwood or Burtville."

"Perfect. This should dovetail nicely then with my Sunday sermon. I'm going to talk about a general remembrance of the dead. But part of the All Saints message is about recognizing saints. I'm going to recognize not only the departed, but the ones walking among us who are doing good."

"That's great," I almost gushed. It was a brilliant way to rope in lapsed Catholics, devout Christians, big donors, as well as his newer more progressive membership.

"It's why I'm talking to you."

"Me?" I had to wonder why he was here. From where I was sitting, it looked like he had everything well under control.

"There is a good marketing opportunity in all this. I'll want you to include profiles of the people we recognize. It will get more people to come in and volunteer with hopes that they're next years' recipients."

"Do you have the list? I can get started on it first thing tomorrow. It's Friday and I'd like to put it in the newsletter in place of something else."

"I'm going to honor Charles and Debra Breaux," he started. "Can you please also think of two blacks or a black couple I can put in there?"

"Um...maybe membership can help with that," I stammered and started wondering if I'd forgotten some important facet of my job that involved knowing a certain percentage of the membership.

"Have you not met any of our black parishioners?"

"Maybe?" I flipped through my memory like it was a Rolodex. "I came to a couple of pot luck dinners and met whomever was at my table."

"Gotcha. Thought you'd have bonded." He took a drink. Was silent for a moment. Closed his eyes. Opened them. "Then do a profile of Catherine Broussard and Antoine Guidry."

I'd taken too big of sips and now I was regretting that I

didn't have any way to take notes. I promised myself to remember this all for the morning. To finish my memo then change up the newsletter before it was due at the printer.

"Are you going to honor them as well?"

"No, the mention should be enough."

Felt a bit slimy, but no doubt he needed everyone's dollars. The honorees were probably bigger donors. Daddy was right, church was a business just like any other.

I tossed back the rest of my drink, then got up to get a glass of water. The only thing I'd had was candy and I could tell the SoCo would eat right through my stomach lining if I didn't dilute it but quick.

"Just to be clear, my assignment is to work up four bios, two on the winners, and two on the honorable mentions?"

"You'll want to run them by Lana just to check for anything that may not fly."

"In the four and a half months I've been here, she's never made any changes. I think the process could be faster if it can go straight from me to the proofreader, then printer," I proposed.

New college graduate. I got it. I'd gone to a good school and good schools before that one. I'd adapted my writing and tone to match the church. After I'd done the dreaded thing I'd never wanted to do, and had taken over much of the damned newsletter, I'd found I was good at that part of the job. It had gone from a throwaway item to collectible. Featuring members and adding a scripture focused advice column had required a doubling of our print run.

"I hear you, Nicole. In areas of communication, I need to make sure there are no subliminal messages going out to the membership."

"Subliminal?"

"I know that people such as yourself might support someone like William Jefferson or Sidney John Barthelemy for example."

"I understand that Baton Rouge is not New Orleans," I said. I'd stayed far away from the third rail of politics and anyone running for office.

"I appreciate what you're saying, but let's keep the systems in place that we have now."

"Got it. Anything else?" I stood and stretched, and threw in a yawn for good measure. It was my cue to get him to leave without outright putting my boss on the spot.

"What are you doing with your free time? Have you met anyone in Baton Rouge?"

That question felt like a trap. The number of acceptable responses probably numbered two. One would have been praying. Two would have been bible study. I hadn't been doing either. Half had been at a few bars meeting a few guys, none of whom I'd brought back here. I'd gone to their place every single time. I couldn't account much for the other half.

"Reading," I answered.

"Proverbs sixteen twenty-seven—"

"Idle hands are the devil's workshop," I responded.

When I saw Collins' broad smile, I realized that I was absorbing more than I thought.

"I like that about you. You're learning. Rosalee was hoping that you could watch the kids this weekend."

"Kids? As in sub for the kid ministry this weekend? I did major in religion, but I'm not qualified for that one. Didn't you once mention that all of the adults in the kid's ministry had to have certification in CPR and have some background in education?"

I was sure of that because I'd done research for an article I'd never published on that part of the church's mission.

"Not the ministry or bible study. You're right. You are in no way qualified for that one. We have to present an image to the public that we take their children's health, welfare, and immortal souls seriously."

"I don't understand..." Drinking must have muddled by brain.

"Our kids. Our regular girl has to go to some kind of family funeral on Saturday."

I tried to hold in my sigh. I'd heard about this kind of thing from friends who were working as personal assistants in New York City. Somehow getting one's foot in the door of publishing or magazines or television also came with duties like picking up dry cleaning and spelling nannies. Not as glamorous as movies made it out to be.

"I don't think I'm the right person. But I'm more than happy to send out some feelers to the congregation. There have to be dozens of teens who'd be happy to help you out."

This wasn't New York. I needed to set the right boundary from the beginning. And unlike entertainment, we had a vast network of women willing to get closer to the associate pastor, and ostensibly closer to God.

"Your sister has two kids, though."

"She knows better than to leave them with me."

"Interesting. I thought you'd be a natural fit, given your background."

I had to talk to daddy and tell him to not volunteer me for stuff. Surely he was behind this. I'd taken the job, that was the totality of what I was willing to do. I wasn't like my mom willing to take on the unpaid labor expected of women. Thank goodness I'd learned those lessons up in Massachusetts in the Women's studies class I'd inevitably ended up taking.

"Sorry. Nope. It's getting late." My words were deliberately clipped.

"Right. I wouldn't want to get in the way of you dressing up as a slutty something or other and heading on down to the river."

"Well, if I'm going to meet my friends, I better get ready," I prompted.

"Do you need a ride?"

"No thanks. I'm good."

"I wouldn't want you to drink and drive. Plus I'm interested in what you're wearing."

"It was only one drink. By the time I'm ready, I'll be sobered up for sure."

"Tell me what you're wearing and I'll get out of your hair."

I sighed. Relented.

"I'm going to be Elvira."

"Mistress of the Dark."

"Not exactly church approved, I know."

"That's a hell of a costume. I don't know if you have enough to hold it up, if I may be so bold."

I wanted to tell him, no not to be so bold, but I held my tongue.

"The makeup will take some time. So will teasing my hair. I'll be completely sober by the time I make it down there."

"If you need a ride back from any bar, you can always call."

"Thanks..."

Collins emptied his glass with a smack of his liquor wet lips. Then he put it in my sink. Collins moved in an unhurried enough fashion that I thought for a second it was slow motion. But he jingled his change and keys, extracted the latter from his pocket.

"I've gotta see the costume."

Reluctantly, I went to the open closet, just a wooden bar between two walls, really, and lifted it out toward him. Collins traced the deep vee that would sit between my breasts. What he'd intimated was right. I was not near anywhere as endowed at the California goth makeup-wearing mistress.

"Lucky guy who gets to take you home and rip this off you."

I knew men thought about sex all the time. Thought about sex with women who were not their wives. But our society was premised upon men not saying the quiet part out loud.

"I'll get those interviews set up in the morning," I said in a chipper voice at the same time I opened the apartment door. This time he took the hint.

SIX

NICOLE

I wish I could pinpoint the moment that what had become a dream job had started to feel like a living nightmare. I kept figuring if I could just work out when that was, I could pivot, do something to make it all go in the right direction.

Associate pastor Seth Collins was a nearly ideal boss. My supervisor, Lana Hawkins had finally become the mentor I'd always wanted. The studio apartment was perfect. Like I'd gotten used to at home and in college, there was even a weekly housekeeper who emptied my trash and scrubbed my floors.

I could walk to work.

Even with the tax of a single person deducted, there was a huge check waiting for me on my desk every couple of weeks. Compared to my friends packed like sardines in tiny New York or Chicago or Los Angeles apartments, eating ramen, and clipping coupons, I was living like someone who worked in finance but without the screaming bosses or ridiculous hours.

On top of that, daddy had announced he was taking a step back from preaching. That his talents really lie in managing the whole operation. He wasn't wrong. Collins's Sunday attendance was quickly eclipsing his own. Daddy didn't seem sad or sorry. I thought as long as he kept his salary and title, he'd be fine.

I should have been deliriously happy with the way everything was going in the purportedly right direction. It's what my high school and college friends insisted when we talked on the phone. I didn't have the heart to tell them different.

Even though it was Thanksgiving Day, I wasn't at home. I was at New Day in my studio's assigned parking space trying to talk myself out of my car and into my apartment.

For a long moment, I sat in my car trying to puzzle through it all. Maybe Seth—he insisted everyone call him Seth—was just a little too involved in marketing and public relations. Though he and Lana Hawkins praised nearly everything I did, and what I missed the mark on was framed with gentle correction, I still felt like I was walking on pins and needles every damned day. Like I couldn't say no to the little requests that encroached on my free time and then spend half my weekends doing.

My belly was churning. I wanted to chalk it up to Aubrey's turkey—deep fried this year. It wasn't that, though. I'd only had a few bites of the poultry or the marshmallow-topped yams. I'd all but skipped the gooey pecan pie, but my stomach was still in knots.

I considered the message my father had relayed to me —again. Seth Collins had summoned me back to Baton Rouge early. There was some urgent outreach that needed to be done so the pews would be full with those who'd come home to their families for the weekend. Collins and my father wanted the main sanctuary to be full to bursting, standing room only.

With a deep sigh, I stepped out of the car and into the steady stream of rain. Precipitation had been falling nearly all day, casting a bleary pall over the celebration at my house. My sister, Michelle, her husband, and her kids had complained all day about the rain.

Apparently, the weather was better in Dallas. I'd resisted telling them if Louisiana was so unbearable, they were more than welcome to return to Texas. Her kids running around and screaming, getting underfoot where Aubrey was cooking and Mam was supervising had given me a pounding headache to go along with the queasy stomach. I should welcome the quiet of being alone, but I didn't.

Once in my apartment, I laid my umbrella in the bathtub, then downed four aspirin, chasing the bitter tablets with the chemical sweetness of Pepto-Bismol.

When that didn't work immediately, I peeled the red seal then opened a bottle of Maker's Mark, got myself some cubes of ice, and poured a few fingers. The cubes clinked so loudly in the glass that I went to my shelf and looked for a relaxing CD or at least one that could drown out my thoughts. At this point in the night, either would do. After a careful perusal, I landed on Sinéad O'Connor.

First, I sat.

Then, I stood.

Next, I paced.

Nothing could shake the combination of adrenaline and dread infused in my limbs. Maybe a bath would work. A long soak with another drink and maybe a book. I went into the bathroom and lit the scented candles that would fill the room with the perfume of lavender.

Lots of the California girls at school had filled their room with the purple blooms in the spring. The smell was supposed to help you relax. People here at home made fun of this kind of stuff.

Admittedly, it all sounded hokey—the yoga, the meditation, and the aromatherapy. But maybe there was something to some of it. Given how I was feeling, I was certainly willing to try anything.

God wasn't the answer. I was learning that lesson every day that I was at New Day. Parishioners...no, that wasn't the word...congregants...members were what we were supposed to call them. Like New Day was some exclusive club they could join.

When the members didn't want to tithe, we assured them God was on our side. When they didn't want to volunteer, we practically promised them a place in heaven. When I'd mentioned public relations to my parents, mainly to get them off my back, it had been no more than a half-baked notion. But this at New Day was exactly the opposite of what I wanted to do.

In my Evolution of Islamic Terrorism class, Professor Shabani told us that the testimony of an allegedly anonymous girl about pulling babies out of incubators was patently false. He talked about how an entire war may have been prevented if the truth had been repeated as much as the lie.

Between that and Tylenol's response to that eighties arsenic scare, pulling their drug business from certain death, I'd been momentarily wowed by the power of public relations to sway opinion. It was only brunch conversation, though. In the future, I'd be way more careful about what I said and who was listening.

The quiet made me look up. I quickly drank down the watered-down liquor.

With the CD stopped, I noticed the sound of knocking on my door. The parking lot had seemed pretty empty. Temporary housing wasn't the kind of place people stayed for the holidays. It wasn't much different than my college dorms during breaks.

Everyone who had someone and could left to spend time with their community. Nevertheless, I stood and slowly made my way to the door, a little unsteady on my feet. I was ready to apologize to whomever I'd probably annoyed with the too-loud music.

"Oh, I wasn't expecting you," I said to the man standing there, his own black umbrella dripping on the corridor's polished concrete floors. My shoulders dropped as the tension eased at the familiar face. "I thought you were going to be an irate neighbor."

"I'm not the least bit irate, Nicole. I just wanted to talk to you about this weekend. When I saw your car in the lot, I knew your father had relayed my message."

Even though my gut was screaming at me not to, I stepped back from the door, letting Seth Collins inside. My unnecessary paranoia every moment I was on campus was driving me crazy.

He'd only taken a few steps before he lifted his golf-sized umbrella.

"What should I do with this?"

"Bathtub," I answered, then pointed toward the lone bathroom in the apartment. Any plans I had to soak in the bath had gone up in smoke like the wax from the candles. Collins headed into the bathroom, then came out without his umbrella.

"Did I interrupt something?" He smiled, then spread his hands apart in a gesture of supplication that was nearly an exact mirror of a statue of Jesus in front of this building. If he were a different person, I'd have thought he were mocking.

"No. Not really. What did you want to talk about? I have a headache and would like to turn in early so I can be prepared for work tomorrow. You want me to come in at nine, right?"

"It's a holiday weekend, so ten would be acceptable. You can sleep in."

I hated when Collins did that: act as if he were the most generous boss the world had ever seen when he was the opposite. Either he was the most pious man on earth or a workaholic or maybe both. I hated that he drove all of us to work at the same intensity as him.

"What's so urgent that we need to come in tomorrow? What time will Lana be there?" Hawkins was a scrupulous boss. She had her own personal fundraising and attendance quotas. She met and exceeded her own monthly goals every time and didn't give a toss what it took to get there.

"No need. I think you've been with New Day long enough to helm this project yourself."

There was the bait. While Hawkins and Collins were excellent at their jobs, they didn't recognize what I'd brought to the table in the five months I'd been there. They often treated me like the red-headed stepchild at the kid's table.

Not a whole lot different than my parent's house a couple of hours earlier. Maybe when Collins left I'd take a hard look in the mirror and figure out what made me so unlikeable or untrustworthy. My dad was larger than life, but I thought once I moved out, and dedicated myself to the job, people would see the real me. What Hawkins and Collins were reflecting back made me very worried about my future relationships and career. I was thinking of quitting sooner rather than later.

"What's the project, Seth? I've already put out the word that this is going to be a Big Sunday." It was the term the New Day higher ups used for the days where tithes and attendance were expected to be double the usual. "And that you're going to have a special sermon ready. People are home during the holidays. From some of the deacons and church board members, I think we'll have the numbers you want to fill the sanctuary."

"Tailgating and television," he announced. "That's the next leap."

"What?"

"I want there to be a massive tailgating party in the parking lot. So that my people can hear the word and maybe enjoy a family barbecue at the same time. Probably a good time to make use of all those leftovers if they don't want to smoke a brisket. And television. I want to be televised. You already did the trunk or treat. Just ten ex that and you'll be a winner."

"Actual television?" I asked. That was a big step up from filling the sanctuary and the adjacent parking lot.

"With Jim Bakker out of the way, there's a huge hole I could fill. I want you to approach cable networks, local networks, anyone with time to spare and get me an hour on Sunday."

Collins was grabbing the vacuum my father left with both hands. The associate pastor paced back and forth in my tiny space as he laid out his plans. He wanted the parking lot filled with loudspeakers. His pulpit wasn't enough.

The five thousand regular churchgoers spread across two services weren't enough. The man's ego had no bounds. It was like he was the sun and everything and everyone spun around his orbit. He'd have been unsufferable if he weren't unfailingly polite. Every request came with a smile, and a pat on the shoulder or back, not a shark tooth in sight.

"You want me to get someone to offer you airtime for free?" That was always New Day's first play. Go hat in hand to ask for what we could easily pay for.

"Free is best, but beggars can't be choosers. I'll pay the asking price for live broadcast."

"Fine. I'll get on all of this first thing tomorrow at *ten*." He did not need me at an early hour. I was thinking I could still get in a bath and a good night's sleep. After the Michelle and family show, I needed both.

"It's late."

I tried to make my glance at my watch subtle yet obvious enough for Collins to get the message. He made no move to leave. When this man was hopped up on enthusiasm, getting him out the door of my office or my studio was like pushing a boulder uphill.

"Can you pour me a drink first? It's raining cats and dogs out there."

"I, uh..." I didn't want to get into the dangers of drinking and driving. His house was on the far side of the New Day campus. Not exactly walkable in this kind of weather without him coming home soaked like a stray dog. Should Collins wrap his Bentley around a tree, I wouldn't want to be on the hook. Maker's Mark *was* ninety proof. Inebriation was right around the corner.

"You can't not offer a guest a drink. I know that your mother and father raised you better than that. How's your dad anyway?"

"You spoke with him today."

My answer was short because my patience was thin. I walked over to my little console table and poured an ounce of the liquid into one of the highball glasses I'd set out earlier. I knew drinking alone was generally a no go, so I usually set out a second glass to make me feel better. It was that one I handed him.

Instead of taking the glass, he wrapped both his hands around mine and the glass. His palms were hot and dry. While I'd normally have drawn back, I hesitated because I didn't want to drop the finger of Maker's Mark. My dad and I had gone to the distillery last weekend and this had come straight off the line. It was a good thirty seconds before he accepted the drink. When he spoke, it took me a minute to catch up with the conversation we'd been having.

"I talked with him only for the minute it took to relay the message. I would not disrespect your mother by keeping J.T. on the phone on a holiday."

"Then, Seth, he's fine. Happy as a clam with the time he has now that he's taken a step back from preaching. My sister and her kids came for a visit and he was pleased as punch to spend time with his favorite daughter and his grandchildren."

The alcohol had loosened my tongue. I just hoped he didn't jump on that comment.

"Are you going to provide grandkids for him?" he asked instead. "That would make for an interesting family Christmas card." Grateful for him overlooking what I'd revealed, I was quick to answer.

"Certainly not now. Anyway, for Sunday I have loudspeakers to set up." It was another hint. I made my glance at my watch obvious this time. It was rounding on ten o'clock. The gray jersey wool dress and black tights that had felt comfortable when I set out for Metairie twelve hours ago were starting to chafe and pinch.

SEVEN
NICOLE
NOVEMBER 28, 1991

"Don't think I didn't notice that you never answered my question a few weeks ago." Collins tossed back his drink without so much as a cough. "Are you seeing someone? Have a boyfriend that you're hiding?"

I had ignored the question because I didn't know why he was asking it. Whether it was his own prurient interest, or because he believed women should be virgins until marriage, or even because he wanted to set me up, I'd wanted none of it.

I'd broken up with my last boyfriend, Christopher Sullivan, right before we'd graduated. Chris and I had gone our separate ways. He and I had promised to move to Boston together, but he'd changed his mind at the last minute leaving me jobless, homeless, and brokenhearted. Over the weekends in Baton Rouge, the attention I'd received from guys had given me confidence in at least one area, that I was attractive enough. Those were not facts I wanted to relive or share.

"There's nowhere to hide anything in this studio," I deflected. "What you see is what you get."

"Can I get what I see?" Seth's pulpit smooth voice had been replaced with something that bordered on seductive.

I blinked.

He had a wife. Everyone knew that. Rosalee had come through the offices more than a few times. There was even talk of giving her a small office next to Seth's for her new "First Lady" of New Day activities and obligations. I might not be a saint, but I did not mess with other women's husbands or my boss or anyone who my family would be embarrassed to see me dating. It's why I kept my weekend escapades to myself.

"What are you asking?" It was the first time I'd spoken plainly. Six months of subtle hints and beating around the bush had gotten me nowhere. Not that he'd ever made a pass or sexually harassed me. He was skilled with his words and everything had been far more subtle than a cartoon villain.

"Do I have to spell it out for you, Kiki, Nicky Mouse? Can I call you one of those?"

"It's Nicole. I..." I trailed off. This part of relating to men never got any easier. They almost always wanted something I was unwilling to give. I tried to figure out the nicest and most oblique way to shut it down. Direct sometimes worked. But direct could get you at best, cursed at, yelled at, slut-shamed. At worst, assaulted.

Men and their capacity for violence was a crapshoot. A

bit likes a Forrest Gump box of chocolates, you never knew what you were going to get. Something in my gut said that while Collins claimed to like straight shooters, demanded it, in fact from his staff, he wasn't ready to hear my honest answer.

"Yes, *Nicole*," he parroted.

"I'm super tired." More deflection.

"How do you like that bed?" Collins pointed toward the purple sugar skull comforter—one of the few things I'd brought from home when it became clear I wasn't ever going back. "Comfortable?" His voice pitched lower the longer he continued to speak. "We bought everything in bulk, so I never got to test out the mattresses."

"A unit just opened up," I said, though it was likely he was already aware. He had an eerily detailed knowledge of everything that happened at New Day, no matter how small. I gestured vaguely outside my own studio. "That pregnant girl downstairs had her baby. Moved in with her aunt in Florida, I heard. You should visit that apartment."

"I don't want to visit that one." His voice was so whisper quiet that I wasn't one hundred percent sure what he said. But his tone caused shivers of fear to run up my spine nonetheless.

Seth Collins stood, hefted his drink, and walked across the room. A place that had felt spacious for one was suddenly claustrophobic for two.

"What was that music you were playing earlier?" His voice was casual. Too casual. He had a wife, even a couple of picture-perfect, cherubic-faced kids that I'd seen walking through church one Sunday. I wanted him to think about them and not me.

"What did your family do today?" I asked, but then I rushed on before he could answer. "Aren't they missing you? I've got everything covered workwise. Why don't you get dessert with them? What's your favorite? Apple pie? Pumpkin pie? Pecan pie? My dad's favorite this time of year is candied pecans. Aubrey makes them sweet and spicy. He can't get enough of that nut. Not my favorite by any stretch, though." My voice petered out. There was an uncomfortable moment of silence before Collins spoke.

"Speaking of nuts..."

Deflection and politeness were getting me nowhere.

"Seth, I'm trying not to be rude here, but I'm tired," I said plainly. "The drive was long in the rain and fog. My niece and nephew gave me a headache. They're lovely, don't get me wrong, but they're toddlers without volume control. Anyway, I just want to take a bath, read for a few minutes, and put myself to sleep before spending the day dialing television stations. So if you don't mind..."

My hint couldn't have been any bigger. I wasn't beating around the bush any longer.

"I love a woman with Southern charm." He tossed back the rest of the amber liquid. Lonely ice cubes clinked against the side of the glass. He put the drink down on the coffee table. Stood. Stretched. Adjusted his tie. Looked ready to give me some much-needed alone time. "You can do all those things now. Sorry to impose."

I nearly groaned in relief. Maybe my gut feeling had been misplaced nerves about something else. My compass could have been the wrong way round. Collins was just a workaholic and maybe a control freak. Without my father around, he was inserting himself into every damned decision about New Day. He was no different than any of the young micromanaging bosses that my college friends complained about. Collins' only difference was that he quoted the Bible more often.

"Thanks for your consideration." Years of charm school made my smile almost genuine.

I stood and went to the little bathroom. The tea lights were still flickering. The tiny candles didn't last long, though. I hoped they'd make it through the bath. I took my own umbrella from the bathtub and stood it in a corner of the bathroom. Then I hefted Collins' out. Shook the rain out the best I could. Wrapped the slippery nylon band around the flaps. I heard his footsteps come from the front part of the studio toward the door. I stepped out of the small room.

"Here you go." I thrust the umbrella toward him, creating a space between us as long as my right arm. "See you tomorrow. Enjoy the rest of your night."

Collins grabbed it into his fist. Tilted the wood handle toward me in a goodbye gesture, then opened my door and walked into the hallway. I pushed the door closed behind him. Turned the deadbolt. When I could no longer hear his footsteps, I slipped off my clothes right there by the door. Didn't bother to put some things in the hamper or hang others in the closet. When I paid my dry-cleaning bill, I'd regret this moment, but that was for later.

Naked, I sat on the edge of the tub, my bum cold on

the white surface, while I waited for it to fill. Tried to reconcile my study of religion with the practice.

Belief was one thing.

Business was another.

Before the bath overflowed, I ran back to the coffee table, poured myself more of the amber alcohol hoping it truly provided the same relaxation I'd seen in the ads at the distillery.

A little buzzed, I was drunk careful so I set the glass on the flat edge of the tub, turned off the water, and slipped under the blanket of lavender-scented bubbles. The relief I'd been wishing for most of the holiday washed over me.

At last.

The sound of the rain was absent in this windowless room. I leaned back and closed my eyes. Whether it was for ten seconds or ten minutes, I couldn't figure out because the next sound I heard was so unexpected that I bolted upright and sloshed water over the edge. The wave took the glass of alcohol with it. It hit the floor and brown liquid mixed with the soap bubbles. Shards of glass went everywhere.

"Let me help you, Nicole," Collins said.

I sat up even further when the cold hit me. As quick as I could muster shame, I crossed my arms over my breasts.

I hadn't been wrong. A key had turned in my lock.

"What...what are you doing?" I tried to sink down and cover myself with what was left of the bubbles.

"I forgot something, I think," Seth said. "Let myself in with the pass keys. Heard the commotion."

I tried to think what he'd brought in with him besides

the golf umbrella. Nothing came to mind other than the sudden chill I felt and discomfort at being naked in the same room as my married boss. New Day may be modern and hip by church standards, but naked girls with married men wasn't something anyone would excuse.

"If you just give me a minute," I sputtered. "Hand me my ro—"

Before I could finish my request, Collins' arms had snaked behind me. One across my back and under my armpits, the other under my knees. Without any apparent effort, he lifted me out. I banded the arm across my breasts again to hide my exposure. With the other hand I splayed it to cover the juncture of my thighs. His loafers crunched on the glass.

Collins carried me to the bed. I hoped he was going to drop me there, run back, and get a towel. The bed part happened, but not the next.

"You're so beautiful," he said. He laid me down like I was made of glass. But he looked at me like I was made of flesh. His hand smoothed my hair from the side of my face. "I was going to go home. Eat a second slice of pecan pie like you suggested. But I couldn't stop thinking about you. How sexy you'd be in the bath." He circled my wrist with one hand. The grip was viselike.

"Seth...please," I pleaded, not sure what I was asking for, but hoping I'd get it.

"Please. That's the word I've been waiting to hear from you. *Please.*"

Every ounce of propriety and politeness left me after his distorted imitation of my words of supplication.

"No. Not please. *No.* I just want to sleep, Seth. Go home before you do something you regret."

He made no move to go back through the door he'd let himself in.

"Let me dip the crane into your oil well. I know that's what you're begging for. Look at your body, hon. Four hundred years ago, you all arrived on our shores and men were lost. Women like you were made for sin. I'll be a saint on Sunday. Tonight I want to be a sinner."

"Please...don't do this," I begged. He was a man of words. Maybe he'd be swayed by mine. My heels dug into the jeweled eye sockets of the skull on my bed. I tried hard to push away from him.

He shook his head very slowly.

"Africa brought us temptation. My flesh is weak. That's Matthew twenty-six, forty-one," he appended as if I needed the source.

"Matthew..." That was the last word I got out before Collins' mouth was on mine. Bourbon and something else was on the tongue that he pushed deep into my mouth. I couldn't look at him.

My eyes flicked up. The ceiling wasn't quite white.

Then they flicked sideways. There was a crack by the window I'd never seen.

Seth's fingers tunneled into my hair, then fisted tight. Pain pricked my scalp. His eyes glazed over with what I assumed was lust. I squeezed my own tight, then went as deep inside my own mind as I could.

"I love these tits," I heard him say before I gasped when he pinched my left breast—hard. "Your nips are dark. You definitely have a more than a little bit of the Creole in you after all."

My eyes opened, focused for a second when I heard his buckle, when he pushed my legs apart, when there was pain inside me like a burn. He pulled out and pushed inside even harder, again, and again, and again.

Then all I could see was the pattern on the ruched curtains. There were ten vertical seams, which means there had to be eleven panels. I'd always gotten straight A's in math.

Collins yelled and grunted at the same time. I could feel his wet penis rub against the inside of my thigh as he pulled out. He blew out a breath and rolled off me on the side toward the wall. I closed my thighs tight, swung them over the side of the bed, pushed my hands against the coverlet, then stood.

When Collins made no move to stop me, I ran to the bathroom. Slammed the door only moments before Thanksgiving dinner came up into the white ceramic toilet bowl. I retched, then flushed three times. My throat was on fire, but my stomach was empty.

I pulled the drain plug, then got in the bath standing up. Wrapped the white curtain around the tub, then turned on the shower. Hot water blasted out. I didn't turn on the cold tap. I stood there, scalded, waiting until the hot water ran out. When I got chilled, I stepped out. Pulled my robe from the hook on the back of the door. I pressed my ear against the thin wood. Listened. There was nothing but the absence of sound.

The rain must have stopped. I didn't know what to do

next, so I put down the lid and sat on the toilet seat and waited and waited until I couldn't wait anymore.

Finally, I tiptoed toward the door and pulled it open. I poked my head around the jamb. It was still silent. I took a step, then a flash of pain like fire seared up my leg. I lifted my foot. Blood was dripping from a jagged cut near my heel.

I'd forgotten about the glass. The one I'd broken when Seth had come back into the apartment. The floor went from white to pink to red and yet, I couldn't move.

EIGHT
NICOLE
NOVEMBER 28, 1991

The throbbing in my foot became so pronounced that eventually, I moved. Putting one foot in front of the other, not caring about the smears of blood on the Pergo floor, I hobbled the twenty feet or so to the dresser that doubled as a TV console table. First, I took out thick sport socks. These were banded with pink stripes at the top. I put on one pair, then added another over them for good measure.

Then I put on clean, white underwear and a brand-new white t-shirt. Navy blue college sweatpants and a matching hoodie completed the uber comfortable outfit. For a split second, I understood my college housemates' tendency to dress down. The last thing I wanted was attention.

I went back to the closet and shoved my feet into my old Stan Smith sneakers, not bothering to squeeze my padded feet into their confines, but smashing down the back of it with my heel so they were more like slippers. I skipped the umbrella. Grabbed my keys and my purse and got down the elevator and into my car as fast as I could so that no one would see me or ask me any questions.

Not until I pulled into the driveway of my parents' home did I realize that's where I'd been headed all along. At every blue and white 'H' road sign, I'd thought about crossing all the lanes to the exit and finding any hospital emergency room that I could so I could ease the pain. The thought of being alone in a cold, sterile waiting room propelled me home. Even if I could go it alone, I needed someone by my side.

After I pulled up the driveway, I was filled with second thoughts and self-doubt. The minute I asked my mother or father for help, they'd have a million questions I wasn't ready to answer. I didn't dare walk through the front door.

Instead, I limped along the slick slate tiles to the kitchen door. Aubrey hardly ever locked it. My mother hated smells in the house, so the garbage can was outside. About ten times a day, Aubrey dumped the kitchen counter's garbage bowl into the rubber trash bin and a locked door was an unnecessary barrier to cleanliness.

The knob twisted easily. The overhead lights were off. For once, I didn't mind the outdated dark cabinets. I wasn't interested in anyone seeing me under the hideous fluorescent light that turned the kitchen a greenish-yellow at night.

I jumped at a gasp. For a moment, I dreaded that my mother or sister was behind that sudden intake of breath between lips. When I turned though, it was just Aubrey. I let every tense muscle go.

"Nicki, you nearly scared the bejesus out of me. I thought you'd gone home already," she said. When it was just us, she was Bree and I was Nicki. She may have been surprised. I was relieved.

Aubrey set down the dirty plates she'd been carrying. No doubt they'd come from my father's or sister's second dessert. The two of them sometimes acted like they hadn't had a meal in days.

I took a deep breath. Let it out. I kept my voice at a whisper. "Bree...I need your help."

"Nicki!" Aubrey didn't follow my lead. Her use of my own nickname was nearly a shout. "You're bleeding!"

"I know." I held a finger up to her lips; our signal that we needed to whisper. "Stepped on glass."

"Where?" she asked her voice barely above a whisper. Her eyes inspected the tile floor as if trying to figure out where she'd gone wrong in her meticulous preparation and cleanup.

"At my apartment."

"And you drove all the way here." She shook her head, but her eyes were soft. Bree may sometimes have snapped at me or chastised me, but the anger or ire never reached her eyes. Those were always filled with love. "Sit. Sit, let me look at this."

When I didn't move, Aubrey crossed the large kitchen and pulled a chair from the breakfast table. It was white wood, upholstered with white damask fabric. I prayed to a God I was starting to lose faith in that I didn't get any blood on it. My mother's ire was never so easily soothed.

"I—"

Understanding was clear on Bree's face. Her head-shake was emphatic.

"Don't worry about anything right now. I'll get this kitchen spotless by the morning. Your mother won't be back in here before then."

I swallowed the lump in my throat. At her gentle urging, I lifted my foot onto a produce box Aubrey had made appear like magic from the pantry. She knelt behind the box and lifted my foot to the bottom of the upside-down crate.

Slowly, she slipped off my shoe. Blood had seeped both layers of my white socks. A single drip escaped from the bottom of my shoe. I followed the blood to the floor.

Aubrey took a breath before she pushed my left pant leg up. Gently she peeled down one sock and removed it. Then did the same with the second. She turned my foot this way and that. She'd done the same all my life. When it came to scrapes and bruises, Bree had been the one I'd gone to.

"What's in here?"

"Glass. A glass broke while I was in the bathtub."

"Don't they have some kind of clinic at that church?"

"It's closed for the holidays." I had no idea if that were true, but New Day was the last place I wanted to be.

"Thanksgiving. Right. Of course."

She extended a single finger, probed at my flesh. I couldn't stop my sharp intake of breath.

"This is deep, Nicki."

"But you can fix it, right? You've bandaged me up more times than I can count."

"That's true, hon. That's true. If it were a tick or a chigger or even a splinter, sure. But this I'm not trained for. There's glass in there that looks like it's at least an inch deep. Plus, it's not clotting. Without that, Nicki, you'll just bleed until all the blood is gone out of you."

"So, what do I do?"

"Not drive another hour for sure. You need to go to the emergency room. Do you want me to get your father? He can drive you."

"No. No, please. Not Daddy." I could hear the desperation in my own voice. "Can you take me? Can Fabien? I can't talk to Daddy right now."

Our eyes met. We communicated without speaking. She went to the bathroom off the pantry and came back with a spool of gauze, most of which ended up stretched tight across my foot.

"I'll go get Fabien," Bree announced, then stood. "We'll carry you to East Jefferson." She disappeared through the kitchen door. Ten minutes later, Fabien came in wearing a green barn jacket.

Without preamble, Aubrey's husband put one arm under my legs.

"Please. Please don't do that. I can walk."

"You can't, Nicole," Aubrey said, her voice sober. "You shouldn't put any pressure on that foot."

Even though I couldn't see it, I knew that Aubrey and Fabien were giving each other the look that said I was going to be a lot of off-the-clock work. I'd seen them do it when my mother insisted on an impromptu scratch dessert for unexpected guests or when my father decided on a Sunday ride in the Jaguar convertible he drove about twice a year, prompting Fabien to have to do a rush detail job and make sure the gas tank was full.

I wanted to not be a pain, but I just couldn't take Mam and Daddy right now. Mam was better than any police detective. She'd have a confession out of me before I could blink. I wasn't ready to acknowledge what had happened.

I'd made a big mistake and I didn't want anyone to know how stupid I had been. My mother had told me from day one that men couldn't be trusted. That I should never be alone with one unless I was ready to have sex with them. I'd violated the rules and paid the price.

I put my good foot down, then tried the other foot. Before I could brace myself, I slipped, then fell.

"Ow! Oh God."

"Can I lift you now?" Fabien was unable to hide his exasperation. I nodded, but then had to look away. He'd probably been up since dawn getting everything ready for my sister's family. In any other situation, I'd have been far more mindful, but I couldn't do that for either of them today.

"Yes. Please carry me to the car," I gritted. "Let's go."

Fabien hefted me and Aubrey scurried alongside.

"East Jefferson General Hospital is the closest, right?" Fabien turned to Aubrey at her question. Both of them were in the front seat of the Jeep. I was laid across the back seat, my leg propped up on a mess of white kitchen towels.

"Just hop on Causeway, it's north of the highway," she said in response to his nod.

Even with the throbbing in my foot, I had to admire Aubrey and Fabien's relationship. I knew he knew where the hospital was. She knew it too. But he didn't yell or roll his eyes or criticize the nervous tic of overexplaining. My own father wouldn't have been as generous.

The car was quiet for the rest of the ten-minute drive. The hospital was brightly lit against the dark and cloudy sky. Fabien pulled into the rotunda, and Aubrey hopped out, then disappeared through the automatic doors.

Not five minutes later, someone in scrubs came out with a wheelchair. All three helped me in. Then I was rolled into the huge lobby that looked more like a hotel than a hospital. The only difference was that the grand piano was empty. As we rolled by toward check-in, I had to wonder who played piano in a hospital. How would that make anyone feel better?

One of them had thought to get my purse out of my car so that Aubrey was able to fiddle through my wallet and produce identification as well as my insurance card. It must have been a slow night, because I was in an emergency room bay soon thereafter. Aubrey stayed by my side. Fabien went to wait or move the car or drive home. I didn't ask which.

"How can I help you?" a doctor who looked as young as my sister asked.

"I cut my foot. Stepped on glass."

"Can I unwrap this gauze?"

I nodded. He was so gentle that I suddenly wanted to cry. I held back the sobs, but tears leaked from my eyes despite my efforts to stop them.

A nurse came in. "Can you take off your sweatshirt?"

"Why?"

"I'm going to need to check your blood pressure. And if we need to run an IV, I'm going to need access. We can get you a blanket if you're cold."

I sat up straighter, leaned forward, and let Aubrey pull the sweatshirt over my head the same way she'd undressed me hundreds of times when I'd been a kid.

Her intake of breath made me look down. There were bruises on my arms. Imprints of Seth's fingers remained. I hadn't remembered him grabbing me so hard.

"How did you get these bruises?" the doctor asked. He'd stopped probing at my foot and instead rolled his stool toward the head of my bed.

"I fell..." I lied.

Fabien stepped in then. The nurse stood quickly and blocked his entrance.

"Sir, who are you? Did you hurt this woman?"

Our groundskeeper glanced quickly between me and Aubrey and the hospital staffers as if trying to quickly assess the situation.

"No," I interjected after I figured out why they were suspicious. He was more obviously black. Aubrey was light enough she could have passed for my own mother. "It wasn't him. These are...they work for my family. They're just here to help. Fabien drove me here rather than doing the whole lights and sirens of the ambulance." I said it like I'd done everyone a favor.

"Okay. Okay." The nurse fluttered her hands in a motion that was supposed to calm us all. "Can you please step out? Please. It's a little crowded. Let me show you where you can wait." She put one hand on Aubrey's back and another on Fabien's. In a moment all three were gone from the room.

"I'm going to give you a pill to relax you." The doctor couldn't quite meet my eyes. "Just a single diazepam tablet. Then I'm going to put a topical numbing agent on your foot, so I can inject you with something that will block feeling in your foot for a little while. I'll pull the glass out, then send you to X-ray to make sure there are no fragments remaining, then stitch it up. You're going to have to be off your feet for about a week."

"I understand," I said.

"I'll be back in a few minutes with a cart. The nurse will be in before that to administer the medications."

Someone else came in with a folded gown. She helped me change out of the rest of my clothes and tie it in the back. She put my clothes in a large plastic bag and placed that on the chair Aubrey had been sitting in. Once she left, I was alone for long minutes. My mind started to wander back to what had happened earlier in the night, and it was all I could do to get it out of that minefield.

NINE
NICOLE
NOVEMBER 28, 1991

I was nauseous and cold on the bed. The pink-and-blue patterned curtains were pulled around me, but I could still hear all the hospital noise, doctors being paged, various beeps and dings from machines.

A woman flicked the curtain and poked her head in. A different nurse, I assumed, or maybe a shift change.

"Can I come in?"

I looked around to make sure she was talking to me. A curtain wasn't a door. I honestly had zero expectation of privacy in an emergency room.

"Sure," I responded.

"I'm Pearl Fleming." After she said her name, I zeroed in on her. She wasn't wearing scrubs, but instead a comfortable-looking pantsuit and pumps. Everyone else was in sneakers or clogs.

"Hello?"

She flicked at the badge on her lapel. "I'm a social

worker here at East Jefferson. I just want to ask you a few questions."

Despite the chill in the hospital's air, I was starting to sweat.

"Oh...okay."

"Where did you get these bruises?"

"Bruises?"

"There's a handprint on your left arm. A bruise ringing your right. There's also bruising at the top of your thighs. Not to mention the very deep cut in your foot. That's a hell of a complicated fall for Thanksgiving. Where were you today?"

"Just home with my parents. My sister and her kids flew in from Dallas. Her husband didn't come."

"Did you get those bruises there?"

"No, of course not. We ate turkey and dressing like always."

"Neither of the people you came in with hurt you?"

"God, no. They work for my family. They live in a house out back. They've been with us forever. I...I...they..."

She held up her hand to stop me.

"The hospital calls me in when there is a suspicion of domestic problems or a crime has potentially been committed. Do you have a boyfriend?"

"No. We broke up in the spring. He's in Boston now. It's why I came home after college." I knew I was talking too much as if words could hide what the bruising on my body couldn't.

"Where do you work?"

"I'm okay. I'm..."

Social Worker Fleming waved her hands in a way that let me know I didn't have to answer anything that made me uncomfortable. Just thinking about New Day and Seth Collins made me twitchy. The thought of the future beyond this moment had me shivering, and not because of the cold air.

"Where do you live, then? If you were home for the holidays?"

"In Baton Rouge. I got a job in the summer and moved there."

Fleming smoothed her clothes, then sat down on the edge of the narrow bed, fitting herself in the space between the plastic guardrails.

"I'm going to ask you a question—" The social worker held up her hand at my immediate and negative reaction. "Before I ask you, there are a few things I want you to consider. First, if you need a place to stay tonight or for a few weeks, that's something I can provide. If you need a restraining order against someone, I can help you get that as well. If something happened to you, you can tell me and what you say will be confidential. I can't tell anyone without your permission.

"Whether or not it's a crime or you choose to prose-cute would be a different discussion entirely. But if some-thing *did* happen to you, then I would like to invite a doctor in here, a completely different team of doctors and nurses, actually, so that they could gather evidence."

I closed my eyes after the word evidence left Fleming's lips. Parish police. Gritty stationhouses. Lineups and courtrooms like I'd seen time and again on television did not paint a pretty picture.

"There would be no pressure to do anything *with* that evidence," Fleming continued even though I couldn't meet her eyes. "If we don't do a thorough examination now, though, then your options down the road may be severely limited. Do you understand everything that I've just said?"

No matter how hard I tried to stop it, I could feel my face crumbling in on itself like one of the rotten crabapples that would collect under the tree outside of my senior dorm room.

"I was...he...raped me." Tears clogged my throat. It took a lot of swallowing before I was able to continue. Fleming didn't huff or do anything but wait patiently. My mind started Monday morning quarterbacking...thinking of ways I could have made the evening go differently. "I made a mistake by offering him that drink."

"You have to know that a crime committed against you was in no way your fault."

That shifting of responsibility had been drilled into me over the last four years. I could wear what I wanted. Drink as much as I wanted. Walk stark naked into a room full of drunk and horny frat boys and I had the right to be left alone. Any woman knew better than that feminist rhetoric, though.

We were solely responsible for our own safety. Men could maybe control themselves, but they didn't.

"He must have thought it was more than it was. But I thought since he was married, he wouldn't think that way."

"Only he is responsible for what he did." It was the same drumbeat I'd heard in women's studies classes. I still didn't believe in the rhythm.

"I can't press charges," I whispered. "He's my boss."

"What were you doing with your boss on Thanksgiving?"

"We're not having an affair or anything like that," I was quick to point out. "He kind of works for my dad. He left a message when I was at my parents' house that there was a work emergency, so I went back. He told me what I needed to do and then I asked him to leave and he did."

I wanted to go back to that moment when I thought I'd achieved freedom from jeopardy. When I thought I'd dodged a bullet. Not the moments after when it became crystal clear that I'd underestimated the danger to me.

"Then what?" Fleming wasn't letting me stay in that space too long.

"Then..." I had to stop because fear washed over me, then a wave of adrenaline. I wanted to run and puke all at the same time. "Then...he came back."

Fleming patted one of my hands with hers. The touch was so tender that I wanted to cry all over again for an entirely different reason.

"Will you allow us to do a sexual assault kit?"

"But you won't tell anyone?" I lowered my voice. This may be confidential, but I could still hear the squeaking of soles on the linoleum as the curtain swished with the human movement. "I don't have to do anything with it, right?"

"No, of course not. I just want to preserve your choices in the future."

"Can you go out in the waiting room? There's a Black couple there. Creole, actually. Sorry. I...it's just that they carried me here. I want them to go home. Tell them I just have to stay for stitches and that I'll get a cab home. They've worked a long day and there's no reason for them to stay around for this."

"Let me set things up with the nurses, then I'll speak with them. You won't regret this."

Pearl Fleming was a liar.

I regretted the decision the moment a woman came in with a big tray of zip-top baggies, paper bags, medical swabs, and a huge speculum. The stirrups from under the bed were pulled out. I had to stick my normal foot into one and my throbbing left foot into the other. I had to scoot down on a bed where the rough sheet only emphasized the cold, unforgiving plastic underneath.

I regretted opening my big mouth when a woman with the bedside manner of a statue swabbed at my mouth and brutally scraped under my fingernails. When she pulled through my hair with the kind of cheap plastic comb they used to sell at the counter of Woolworth's, I wanted to scream.

I regretted everything I'd done over the last months when a doctor didn't so much as announce he was slipping the heavy, freezing metal instrument into my private parts. I didn't know until then that cold could burn.

The flash from the camera was the worst. No one had taken pictures of my nude body since I was a baby that I could remember. This woman held the camera close to me.

Flash.

One bruise was captured.

Flash.

Another was memorialized.

Flash.

Someone would have a picture of the handprint on my left arm, the black and blue and yellow marks on the other.

It was more than an hour and a half before the ordeal was over. Only then did the original emergency room doctor and nurse come back. They were noticeably subdued when they added the promised topical ointment, then injected something that made me more numb and colder than I'd been before if that were even possible.

It was nearly one in the morning when all was said and done. After some consultation just outside of my hearing, I was admitted to the hospital. Someone gathered what was left of my stuff that hadn't been bagged and tagged as evidence and rolled it and me to a single room. I got an extra blanket, someone turned up the heat, and despite the light and noise, I fell into a deep sleep.

TEN
NICOLE
NOVEMBER 29, 1991

Every part of my body was heavy with exhaustion even though the sunlight streaming through the thin curtains indicated morning had arrived. I hadn't thought I could fall asleep. Now I didn't want to wake up.

"Bree?" It was a lot to keep my eyes open. But I was sure I'd seen our housekeeper between my lids.

"It's me, Nicki." She reached out from the chair that she must have pulled up to the bed and held both my hands in hers. "How are you feeling?" Her voice was soft with sympathy. "I'm surprised they kept you. Must be a deep cut."

Whatever will I'd had to keep my eyes open left me. I tried to turn my head away, but the tears were leaking out before I could hide them. Keeping secrets from Aubrey wasn't something I'd ever been practiced in.

"What aren't you telling me? Nicki, please talk to me." The rest she didn't say, but didn't have to. If I told her anything, it would be our secret. We must have had hundreds of them between us through all these years. I probably didn't remember half.

For as long as I could remember, that's just how it had been between us. My mother's favorite was Michelle. My father's favorite was himself, then maybe me. I'd always had Bree.

"You know how I started that new job..."

"At New Day of course. Of course. Fabien caddied for them on the day they arranged it."

"His name is Seth. Seth Collins. I...he came over last night."

"To your new apartment?"

"I didn't invite him or anything," I backpedaled. "But he's my boss, so I didn't think I could say no. He's one of those people who has ideas twenty-three of twenty-four hours in a day and always has to share them immediately."

"Okay."

"I was having a drink and getting ready for a soak in the tub. Just trying to relax after Michelle and the kids. No offense, but they kind of gave me a headache."

"Me too...a little." Bree's eyes flicked guiltily. Don't tell your mom, she didn't have to say. I mirrored her sheepish smile.

"So, I felt like I had to give him a drink, you know. It felt impolite to be sipping from a glass and not offer him something."

Bree nodded her understanding. Southern culture was no joke. If I'd been anything but polite, it would have gotten back to my father faster than the speed of sound. A rebuke from him or my mother about bringing shame upon my family wouldn't have been far behind.

"Seth drank his bourbon while telling me our worship this weekend needed to be a bigger event than the Cowboys–Steelers game. He talked for a long time, then when he'd finished talking and drinking, he left."

Bringing up this memory was horrible, because that moment I'd felt safe had been no more than an illusion. I wanted to turn back the clock, flip back the calendar just one day so I could get in my car, or do something other than remain in my studio like a sitting duck.

"Was he inappropriate?"

"Maybe. Not really. I can't say. I just felt kind of uncomfortable. He was like kind of hyper. But he gets that way. Maybe he's got a direct line to God or something. Guys like that always seem to be running at one hundred miles an hour. So when I closed the door behind him, I just got undressed and turned on the taps in the bath."

"Then what, Nicki?"

"Bree..."

"Everything is better if you talk about it. How many times have I said that to you?"

I sighed.

"A thousand."

"Was I ever wrong?"

I shook my head. She never was. Bree had stayed up with me all night when my high school boyfriend dumped me after I'd lost my virginity to him on prom night the week before. When Christopher moved to Boston without me, she'd been there. For other stuff too, not just boy stuff.

It was always hard to talk at first. To admit that I wasn't wanted or that I'd made some embarrassing mistake. Then, I'd cry and Bree would often make me laugh. She always made me beignets. We'd stay up too late, laughing and crying, high on powdered sugar.

"No, you've never been wrong." Sobering memories from last night flooded through my body, obliterating those other happier ones from the past.

"Tell me."

"He came back." That had come out in a whisper. Shame billowed around me in a cloud of heat.

I could practically feel the next question bursting from her: Why had I let him back in? I needed her to know that I wasn't that stupid.

"He has a key."

"To your apartment?" Her face scrunched up in disbelief.

"To everywhere in New Day. He just lets himself in wherever we are on campus. The door opened. I was trying to figure out if I'd heard what I thought I'd heard, when he appeared in the bathroom doorway. He dragged me out of the bathtub. It wasn't exactly like my clothes were there to stop him, make him think twice. Then, when I didn't give him what he asked for, he took what he wanted."

Aubrey nodded in such a way that I knew she understood exactly what I was talking about.

Like she had when I was five and even when I was

fifteen, she climbed up in the too-small bed and hugged me. I resisted at first, because I wasn't a baby anymore, but then I took a deep breath of her unique scent and I gave in. She smelled the same as she always had, like lemon verbena. I let her hold me while I let out a few tears, just enough to keep the deluge at bay.

The door to the room opened suddenly. For once, I didn't care what anyone thought of me and Bree. I didn't move. She did, though. Too often we'd been chastised for being too close.

"Sorry to interrupt you and your mom. I can come back."

Mom? Something about that word arrowed its way inside me. Didn't feel as alien as it should. I shook away that feeling. Obviously, this stripping of my veneer had made me vulnerable to fantasies long buried. They needed to go back into the graveyard of my mind. This thing with Seth Collins was going to need a crypt all its own.

"She's not..." I didn't finish because guilt closed my mouth. There'd been a lot of times, especially when I was a kid, that I'd wished Bree were my mom. She'd always loved me like I thought a mom could. But the nurse wasn't here for all that.

"I have your antibiotic shot, here. I just need to confirm your height and weight."

"She's five foot seven. One-forty," Aubrey answered.

I nodded in confirmation.

"This is going to be an intramuscular shot. It's a prophylactic that will address any possible sexually trans-mitted diseases you may have been exposed to."

The room was quiet as no one moved. A fleeting smile graced the nurse's face. "Intramuscular means I need you to flip over so I can give you the shot in your buttocks."

"Oh, okay." I flipped. The gown opened just at that moment revealing the exact area that needed to be poked. Aubrey had moved, but she still held my hand in hers while the nurse swabbed with alcohol, then jabbed me and pushed down the plunger. It was over in seconds, and she and her tray of paper and plastic debris was out of the room before I could lie prone again.

"No dignity in hospitals," Aubrey observed.

The door opened again, and it was the social worker, Pearl Fleming.

"I need to talk with you about a couple of other issues." She sent a meaningful glance toward Aubrey. I remembered then that I'd had her and Fabien sent home last night.

"It's okay if she stays," I said. "I told her everything."

"First things first. Do you want an STD test panel?"

My mind reeled. What Seth had done was one thing to deal with, but getting a virus that led to a disease with a death sentence had never crossed my mind.

"You should do it, Nicki," Aubrey said sensing my hesitation. "It's always better to know something than to not. Gives you a way to prepare for what you're going to have to handle."

"I...fine."

Fleming produced a clipboard I hadn't seen and asked me a series of probing questions concerning my sexual history and about drug use. I tried not to squirm—to be matter-of-fact in my approach to the answers. I couldn't imagine anything as embarrassing as all of this ever happening to me again. Not after last night when someone had photographed my private parts.

"It's very likely that unless you've been involved in any other risky behaviors, you'll test negative this time. But because of how HIV behaves, you'll need to schedule another appointment in six months. Also, is pregnancy a possibility?"

I shook my head, grateful for one decision I'd put off.

"I'm still on the pill."

Aubrey shook my hand gently, then she turned her eyes toward Fleming.

"What are the other issues?" I asked after it had been determined that the hospital wouldn't need any more blood. They had drawn enough the night before to test for everything.

"Do you want to report what happened to you?"

"Like police and the court and all that?" Aubrey asked.

"Yes, all that," Fleming affirmed.

"What would be involved?" I asked. I had zero plans to report a damned thing. But I wanted to make it look like I'd considered all the angles before I gave my denial.

"We'd call in the East Baton Rouge Parish police. They'd take a report, your version of what happened. Then we'd hand off the physical evidence we collected. They'd interview the...man who did this to you." Fleming's empty hand was flapping about. It was the first time she seemed awkward. Her obvious discomfort solidified my decision to end it right here.

"After that," Fleming continued, "they'd possibly make an arrest and decide what charges to file. He might be offered and accept a plea. He might not and then there'd be a trial. You'd get the opportunity to face your assailant," she finished, trying to put a positive spin on the idea of detailing what Seth had done with me—*to me*—in front of a courtroom full of people. Those selfsame people would also be looking at full-color pictures of my bruised and naked body.

No, thank you.

"I'll think about it," I said. I accepted the folder she gave me along with her business card. I flipped it open briefly to see that the thick fold of paper held glossy pamphlets from all sorts of agencies. The women on them all had sad, tearful faces. I was not in any rush to join that group.

"I'll tell the doctor on call that you're ready for discharge."

"Thanks."

"Oh, do you have somewhere to stay?"

My eyes met Aubrey's. She knew like I did that my studio probably wasn't safe. Not unless I changed the locks or got some other kind of barrier to entry.

"I'm not sure," I said. Making a case to my parents to move back home without an explanation wouldn't be easy.

"You mentioned that you lived in Baton Rouge. I know that you may not be religious or anything, but I'm sure you're familiar that some nonprofits are church-based."

"Catholic Charities and all that," I said while nodding

and trying not to speculate on the women's shelters supported by the church. More sad and tearful women's faces.

"Our protestant churches are stepping up to the plate with government support of faith-based organizations. New Day is an up-and-coming church that offers studio apartments to those in need of a safe place to stay. Their information is in the packet. Seth Collins, the pastor there, has been a force for good in the community, so I'd seriously look into that if you're not safe to go home."

"Thanks so much for your help," Aubrey said when shock stole my voice. Fleming's nod was grave as she left the room.

A chill came over me again. There was no safe place for me. I had no idea where I'd go when they discharged me.

ELEVEN
NICOLE
DECEMBER 2, 1991

"Missed you at this weekend's service," Seth Collins said.

I froze with my back toward the door of the office I shared with my boss. I'd thought I was alone.

For some amount of time I couldn't count, there was no sound. It was as if I'd walked into a vacuum. I couldn't breathe, either. Maybe there were black holes right here on earth. My head spun as I tried to figure out how to make myself unstuck. This had to be a panic attack. No one died from them, even if I felt like I would right at this moment.

I closed my eyes.

When I opened them again, I was able to see and hear and breathe. It would be enough to get through this moment. After that, I'd put one foot in front of another again and again until I was able to walk out of here. My resignation letter was written. I'd come in early to type it out on the Selectric in the receptionist bay.

My plan had been to get to my office.

Get some letterhead.

Type out the letter.

Get it to Seth's assistant.

I'd hoped to do it all before he came to work. Make myself a ghost.

"I had to go to the emergency room," is what I said when I found my voice.

"I heard."

"From who?"

"Pearl Fleming."

If I'd eaten anything in the last three and a half days, I'd have lost it on the industrial carpet under my office chair.

"Flem-flem-ing," I stuttered.

"Got a call in the middle of the night that someone'd been hurt. Needed a place to stay that was safe. You know how much I've dedicated our church to the task of keeping those in need safe from the streets."

"I c-c-cut my foot," I stammered out an excuse. It had the benefit of being true.

"Seth, Nicole called me about missing work this past weekend. I had it covered. Ratings are in," Lana Hawkins said as she walked into our office area. There was a curl of fax paper in my boss' hand.

Collins' eyes shifted from me to Hawkins and then back. I squirmed in my seat, then rustled some papers to make it look like I was doing something. Anticipation stole the spotlight from me.

"Your ratings were better than *Buckskin Bill*," Hawkins announced. She waved the thermal paper in emphasis.

"Praise the Lord." Collins threw up his hands as if the hands of God were about to meet his in communion. "We're reaching them. Our church will grow in the glory and sight of God."

Hawkins handed the faxed page to me. I scanned the list of shows over the week and saw that our ratings were better than the Saturday night local news. He was right. It was that good *for him*.

"More than ten percent of the local audience was tuned in to your Thanksgiving weekend sermon," I added. Collins' face was still turned toward the ceiling. Tears welled under his lids. Even I was thinking God was in the room with us. A bolt of lightning or a booming voice wouldn't have startled me.

As if on cue, my phone rang. Not wanting to meet Collins' eyes, I grabbed at the receiver. After I answered with my name and title, the caller identified themself. It was a reporter from *Politic*, one of the nation's top-three weekly news magazines. They were looking to feature our fearless leader. If Seth Collins accepted the offer, the promise was that he'd be on the cover. Even the lowliest assistant knew what that could mean.

I punched the hold button and brought the handset to my chest.

"You might be in the running for American of the Year." For the first time that morning, I met Collins' eyes.

"The cover?" Hawkins asked, her eyes going wide as I turned to her.

"National cover," I replied matter-of-factly.

"That'll be a hell of a thing to add to your résumé," Collins added. It was ambiguous enough that he could have been talking to either of us, but for me, the message was direct and clear.

If I talked.

If I reported him.

If I said anything about what had happened on Thanksgiving night, then I'd lose not only my job, but any chance I had at getting a good reference. The work I'd done to put Seth Collins at the top of the megachurch race for dominance would be for naught.

I shooed them away, then punched the phone. It only took a few minutes to secure the interview and Seth Collins' place in the annals of American history. It took less time than that to seal my fate as a woman who would take her very dark secret to the grave.

TWELVE
NICOLE
DECEMBER 23, 1991

"God's Right Hand."

Those were the words emblazoned on the glossy front page of *Politic* magazine next to a grainy black-and-white shot of Seth Collins. The early copy of the magazine stared at me from my car's passenger seat as I drove from Baton Rouge to Metairie.

Daddy had summoned me for Christmas Eve. I was getting a one-day jump on the traffic and avoiding all the holiday rigamarole at New Day. Hawkins may not have been happy, but Collins smoothed over my absence. I swerved to avoid a crater-sized pothole in the road and the magazine slid across the seat as if it were taunting me.

Politic was the third-most-popular news magazine in circulation after *Time* and *Newsweek*. That meant five point four million people would see Seth Collins' black-and-white countenance staring at them from their doormats, and mailboxes, and newsstands, the editorial board's choice practically proclaiming to twenty percent of America that he was the second coming.

Add to that Collins' full schedule of interviews I'd booked on the networks' Sunday morning shows and cable news and he'd have nearly full penetration of America this month. He'd already had full penetration of me. Now the rest of the country and I would have something in common. Under my breath I laughed at my droll humor.

If I were a better woman, I'd have quit my job. Instead, I'd given a rapist a nationwide audience. I was better at my job than I'd ever suspected I would be. My father had always been a good judge of character. He's been right about me, if not about Collins.

"How's your foot?" my mom asked when I walked through the back door and into the kitchen of my parents' house. I hoped that it would only be Aubrey. But my mother, sister, and housekeeper were there. It was way more of a welcoming committee than I expected or wanted. It wasn't my house anymore, though, so I had to make nice.

"It's good, healing. What are you doing?"

Out of the corner of my eye, I could see Aubrey shucking oysters next to already chopped ingredients for dressing on the other side of the kitchen.

"Before you surprised us, we were trying to decide if we're going to drive to Lafayette for the Window Wonderland. We were planning to pick you up along the way."

I heard the slight behind the words but ignored it. It

was impolite to turn up unannounced, but I'd kind of hoped they would have already left before I got here. Every year they had the same debate, and every year they left late with only minutes to spare. I'd wanted to get here, clean out the guest room, and get situated so I could put on my armor and get ready for another happy Long family Christmas. *Happy* were the only kinds of holidays we were allowed to have.

"I'm out," I said. I laid my keys on the counter in emphasis. "But you should go."

"What's that in your other hand?"

I dropped the early-release issue on the kitchen counter, glossy cover facing upward, my biggest career accomplishment so far, there for the world to see.

"Oh my gosh, is Seth Collins *Politic's* American of the Year?" my sister squealed her question. She snatched up the issue and thumbed to the article which featured more pictures and column inches. Seeing that smiling face turned my stomach. I had to look away.

"That's a hell of a coup, Nicole. You'll be able to go anywhere your heart desires after this. Maybe New York or even Boston if you and Christopher ever consider giving it another try," my mother added.

"Mam, that relationship is in my rearview mirror." If she liked Christopher so much, *she* should date him.

"Never say never." My mother actually lifted and wagged her manicured finger. I wanted to grab it and bend it back until she screamed in pain.

The flash of violent thought scared me. Made me even

more nauseous. Since Thanksgiving, I'd had more moments like that than I wanted to admit. I was becoming as depraved as the man who had hurt me.

"Aren't you so excited that you can say you knew Seth Collins when?" Michelle gushed. "If I were you, I wouldn't be making any plans to leave. What was that about anyway, wanting to leave?"

"I was just coming home to take a few months to decide what I wanted to do. Think of it as half a gap year."

Six months that I deeply regretted but couldn't change. In my mind, while I made the three-day journey from Hadley to Metairie, my plans had seemed so simple. All I wanted was to heal from Christopher's betrayal in a place that didn't remind me of him. We'd never taken walks here, or made plans here, or slept together here. I thought home was going to be a safe space to figure out what my life would be like without him in it.

During college, every plan I'd made had been about Christopher and *his* future. Unspoken was that I was signing up to be a tagalong spouse. My mother had done it. My sister was doing it. Until he'd ended our relationship, it had been a fair trade-off. I got love. He got my unending support. No one expected future leaders of America to buy their own sheets or sign up for utilities.

"Then you were going back north, right?" My sister, Michelle, had that laser focus on me that made my stomach do flips. She was the original mean girl who always struck with unerring precision. I did everything I could to stay away from her. Someone always got hurt. Most of the time it was me.

"It's where the jobs are, where most of my friends are." I was almost ashamed at how quiet my voice was becoming. Just like that night with Seth Collins, this wasn't about anything more than survival.

"But not where your family is." My sister's headshake was overly dramatic. My parents made no comment. I looked between them, then kicked myself for expecting something different after all these years. "Went to school up north and we stopped being good enough for you?"

"Michelle, that's a lot of drama," I protested. My sister was best diffused like any bully—head-on. "I just want a change of pace. A chance to try something new. There's no crime in that."

"You think I'm a loser for getting married and moving to Texas, don't you? Those northern girls don't do anything like that."

"Michelle. I'm not sitting in judgment of you. We're different people with different paths in life. That's all."

"Do you talk to Christopher?" my mother asked. Something in her tone was desperate. Desperate to stop an argument between me and Michelle? Desperate to get me married off and out of her house?

Damn the holidays.

This is why I didn't always want to come home. Why I didn't want to stay here even if they'd allowed me to stay. No one with eyes in their head would deny that my mother and sister had some special relationship that was never expansive enough to include me.

My old room now had pictures of my sister's wedding, her kids right after birth, her and her husband on vacation. There wasn't a single one of me. For years Daddy had said that it was because I was born second and sometimes later kids get less attention. At least that's what he'd said when I'd asked why Michelle had a fully fleshed out fifty-page baby book and I had...nothing.

Somehow, I was the black sheep, though I could never figure out what in the hell I'd ever done wrong. Believe me, I'd tried. Daddy treated us way more fairly. My mother, though, never.

I tried to catch Aubrey's eye. It's what I always did in these moments. Usually, she nodded or gave me some signal of support. It's what kept me from feeling alone in my own family. But tonight, our housekeeper never looked up from the cutting board in front of her.

Shame flooded me. Aubrey probably thought I was some kind of stupid slut for allowing Collins to do what he'd done to me. My mind whirled as I tried to think of where I could go. Where I could find some solace or acceptance or just a moment to work through what had happened.

"Christopher's the best you could do, you know," my sister hissed. "If anyone knew the truth about you, they wouldn't want to be with you anyway."

All I'd done was put Seth Collins' face on the kitchen counter. He hadn't raped any of *them*. There was no reason I could pinpoint for what was happening, where the sudden anger had come from.

"Michelle Margaret!" I hadn't seen my father come in. Relief flooded through me. He would stop my sister and mom from beating up on me. He had car keys in his hand. Maybe he was driving to Lafayette and not Aubrey's husband. It didn't matter. In about ten minutes they'd all be out of here and I could have a moment to breathe.

"What, Daddy? Why are you keeping it a secret? Nicole should know what we know."

It was as if I was falling into a void. Nothing was making sense. I stalked toward Aubrey. Pulled the knife out of her hand brandished it.

"You told them?" I accused her.

"I didn't say a word," Bree said before she snatched the knife back. But she wasn't looking at me or chopping vegetables. She was looking right past me and at Daddy.

"What? What are you hiding now?" Michelle screamed. "Are you having an affair with Seth Collins? I've thought there was something off with you and him from the moment you got that job and moved over there."

"I moved out because Mam turned my room into a craft room," I said weakly. I was so tired of defending myself, trying to protect myself. It was something I wasn't good at obviously.

"So what's the secret you told Aubrey?"

"I was...attacked," I sobbed. It had been so hard to keep all that inside. It all burst forth like water through a breach in a levee.

"What do you mean attacked?" My mother came toward me. Shoved up my blouse sleeves as if she were looking for bruises. They would have been there last month but had since faded from purple to green to yellow. The pastor's ugly handprint was gone.

I didn't answer. My throat was closed as if it were superglued. I couldn't say it out loud.

"She was raped, right there at New Day. At your church in Baton Rouge," Aubrey said. Her voice was loud and clear, not a single tinge of its usual obsequiousness. The silence that followed was deafening.

"Do you need to go to the hospital?" That was my mother.

"No," I finally spoke up for myself. "I went."

"When?" my sister asked, an accusing finger wagging.

"Thanksgiving," I said.

"The night you cut your foot?" I could see my mother's face screw up as she tried to work out a timeline.

"I cut my foot trying..."

"I'm going to kill him." The keys in my father's hands flew toward the wall.

"Daddy, please," I begged. "No one needs to go to jail over this."

"He does. If someone at my church did what you're saying, then he needs to be locked up."

"Did you call the police?" Mam asked.

"The hospital social worker made them take evidence. Told me I could make a decision later."

"And your decision was to go back to work? How stupid is that?" my sister piled on. "Is it one of the workers?" My mother asked. "Only the people that came after your dad got there have had background checks."

"I bet you she's making it up." Michelle looked between my mother and father waiting for the usual backup. "You came up with this excuse because you got caught having an affair, didn't you? Is it some married man there?"

"Michelle!" My father's voice was uncharacteristically harsh.

"What. Someone's got to tell it like it is. I'm so tired of all the secret keeping."

My stomach twisted, and for the first time in weeks, it wasn't related to Seth Collins or New Day.

"What are you trying to say, Michelle?" I turned on my sister. "Just spit it out. I'm so sick and tired of all your stupid fucking innuendo. What favorite-child card are you waiting to play? Show your hand. It's truth time."

"Did you ever wonder why you don't have blond hair?"

"What, I'm adopted? That's the card you're playing? Loser hand, sis. That's just like you. You've always said stupid shit like that. Which I'd have believed if I didn't look like Daddy."

"Michelle, stop it. Stop this. Grow up." My mother's face was turning scarlet. Aubrey looked like she'd seen a ghost.

This wasn't about me going to school up north.

This wasn't about Christopher dumping me.

This wasn't about Seth Collins.

This was what a family looked like before it imploded.

There was a part of my brain that wanted to freeze this moment forever because there was about to be a before and an after. If I could stop time, I'd have used the power on Thanksgiving when I really needed it.

"That's just it, Mam, Daddy. I *am* a grown woman."

"Michelle!" My mother was screaming. A Southern

woman did not raise her voice, but a tornado of sound had swirled around all of us, nevertheless.

"Mam isn't your mother, Nicole."

We all jumped when Aubrey dropped the knife she'd been using. The sound of hardened steel on ceramic tiles reverberated through the room.

My sister may have told a lot of mean lies most of my life. She had thrived on hurting me. This had the ring of truth, though. I could feel that with my whole body.

Aubrey never picked up the knife. She snatched off her apron and ran out of the back door. More of the truth came crashing down on me like a shit ton of bricks.

"I thought Theriot was a family name," I whispered. Given the unspoken intertwining of Black and white families below the Mason-Dixon line, I had never asked too many questions about it. The first time I'd pointed it out, my mother had gone white and my father quiet. After that, I'd mostly left the subject well alone.

My father looked at me, then his wife, then followed Aubrey out of the back door.

"It is," Michelle said. Her face held vindication, and I'd never hated those little doll features more. "It's your mom's last name."

And Aubrey's.

So much that had been murky from my early childhood was clearing as if a smokescreen had been lifted on my past. The door banged against the stop so hard, it splintered from its anchor on the wall. No one moved to pick up the pieces. There wasn't going to be any time to consider any of that, to sort through memories.

"Button your coat, Nicole," my father commanded. For a long second, I thought he was going to kick me out. I steadied myself for whatever was to come next.

"Why?" My voice was mouse squeaky.

"We're going to the Baton Rouge Parish police."

THIRTEEN
NICOLE
DECEMBER 23, 1991

Before I could protest, my daddy bundled me into his Cadillac and was roaring off the property when I hadn't even clicked my seat belt. The first ten minutes of the ride were dead quiet, the only sound the faint whomp of the tires on pavement. It was the first time I regretted that the car was nearly sound-proof. A little wind noise would have been welcome.

I spoke before my dad did. The last thing I wanted to talk about was Seth Collins. The second to last Aubrey Theriot. But I wanted answers more than I wanted comfort.

"Bree?" I whispered my question. There were so many others, none appropriate. I knew how the birds and the bees worked. When I was about fifteen, I'd walked in on Daddy and...Mam. There wasn't enough mind bleach to get that memory out, but I'd made peace with the fact that they'd had sex at least three times. Now I was dialing back that number and a new mental image was taking its place.

"Your mother...Margaret and I were going through a tough time. Aubrey...she's a good listener. One thing led to another..."

"I know where babies come from, Daddy." I had to swallow the feeling of rejection before I could get the words past my lips. "Why didn't Bree keep me?"

The question would have been better put to Aubrey herself, but she wasn't here to answer for her crimes. My father was.

"By that time, your mother'd had a few miscarriages. Michelle was more of a miracle than we'd ever realized." I bit my lip. My bitch of a *half*-sister was not the definition of a miracle. "The doctors said your mother wouldn't be able to carry another baby to term. Secondary infertility was what they called it. Margaret was devastated. Aubrey has lived at the estate her whole life. Her mother lived there and her mother before."

Without the historical context of successive generations of women working for a single-family sometimes going back to before the Confederacy, none of this would make any sense. I would have been hard-pressed to explain any of it to most of the girls I went to college with. In fact, I never did.

"What did you say that would have made her give me to Mam?" That last stuck in my throat like thick peanut butter. I had to swallow hard just to breathe.

"I'm...I'm not proud of this."

"What? What aren't you proud of?" My mind spun out very far. My father lived life balls to the wall. It was the

Texan in him. He lived big and unapologetically. Regret wasn't a word in his vocabulary.

"Aubrey was young, and her mom was sick."

"Please tell me you didn't pay her for a baby. Slavery ended over a hundred years ago."

"We did not pay her. Your mother laid out a very convincing case for having us raise you and not a single mother living on a housekeeper's salary."

"What was the lynchpin?" There had to be something compelling enough to separate a mother from a child. Money wasn't enough.

"That we'd raise you as white."

I sat back so hard, my head bounced off the headrest. Now that, I hadn't seen coming. Because of course, how I'd seen myself wasn't how I was...anymore. I'd lived in Louisiana my whole damned life. Four years in Massachusetts hadn't erased my understanding of the very strict rules that governed life down here.

Specifically, the one-drop rule.

No one would say it out loud anymore. It wasn't politically correct, but it still applied. I could do what others did and call myself French or Creole or whatever, but last night I'd gone to bed white.

Tomorrow, I'd wake up Black. I flipped down the visor. My skin was still pale, my eyes blue, my hair straight and inky black. The genes expressed weren't what made up the building blocks of me.

My head pounded with the reassessment I'd have to make about everything in my life. Is that why Christopher had broken up with me? Had he seen what I couldn't?

Had Seth Collins known about me? Seen me as an easy mark? A Black woman he could do anything to without repercussion?

I don't know how long I was quiet before I noticed Daddy's car was coming to a stop. We were under a huge overhang that wouldn't have been out of place in any large hotel. The building itself was a huge block of windows and concrete. The squared-off edifice did not evoke empathy.

Baton Rouge Police Department was emblazoned above the portico.

There was no valet, but Daddy turned off the car under the portico anyway. He was not a man who spent time looking for his own parking spaces.

"Let's go, Nicole." The bark was an order.

"Do you think this is a good idea?"

"That man has to pay. He's not going to get away with defiling my daughter. Not today."

After I glanced at the car he'd parked with impunity, I sucked in a very deep breath and followed him through the automatic doors.

"Can I help you?" a bored-looking man asked, who was for sure younger than me.

"I need to talk to a detective." My father's voice was a command of instant respect. The young officer stood quickly, snapped to attention.

"For...sir?"

"My daughter was violated."

The man's face turned crimson as he averted his eyes from mine.

"Let me call up to Sex Crimes."

My own face would be that color soon if I didn't get a moment. I stalked down a corridor following signs for the lavatory. After I squeezed something out of my bladder, I washed my hands, then patted at my cheeks with damp palms.

Under the flickering fluorescent lights I stared at my face. How could I be so different, but look the same? All of Seth's comments hit me then. He'd known the thing my sister had known, my entire family had known. Was I the only person in the dark?

I was coming out of the ladies' room, when a man in a brown suit exited the elevator. From across the lobby, I watched my father introduce himself and shake the police officer's hand. They talked for a minute while I watched. Only when they turned in my direction, did I start back across the tiles toward them.

"Nicole? Let's go up and have a talk in a conference room."

I shook his hand and followed them up. Someone got me water and I got as comfortable as I could in a wooden chair.

"I'm Detective Neil Bowers. I've been in Juvenile and Sex Crimes for about four years. I'm going to have to ask you what happened. It's going to be uncomfortable, but this won't be the last time you have to tell your story."

I covered my eyes with my hand. Took a deep breath. Put my hands in my lap. Sighed.

"Oh, okay."

Bowers slid a pad of paper toward himself. Clicked a

ballpoint with his left hand and started writing something.

"Tell me your name, address, age."

"Nicole Theriot...Long. I'm twenty-two." I gave him my address. Bowers' frown was immediate.

"Metairie is a long way from Baton Rouge."

"I'm sorry. Habit. I'm actually living here now." I gave him the street and apartment number for my studio at New Day.

"Alrighty then..." Bowers trailed off, then turned and cupped his hand to my father's ear. Daddy patted me on the back, then left the room. He came back in with an awkward half-smile on his face. Seeing me see it, Bowers quickly rearranged his face into something more somber and appropriate.

"You're living at New Day, huh." He snapped the thumb and middle finger of his right hand. Your dad, James Long, is J.T. Long? Man, I didn't recognize him." He blushed in a way that said my father wasn't his flavor of pastor. "You must have met Seth Collins? Now that he's preaching most of the time....He's done us proud here in Baton Rouge. I think one day he'll preach the word of God to as many people as Jim Bakker did or even Pat Robertson. That sermon he did on the Sunday after Thanksgiving is exactly the thing that we all needed to hear."

His words were like a fist to my gut. The chair scraped against the floor as my body slumped against the wood that curved around my back.

"What I'm going to ask you now may make you uncomfortable, but rest assured I've heard everything. I won't be shocked or surprised or embarrassed. So let's start at the very beginning. Do you know the first and last name of your attacker?"

If I could have slipped all the way down to the floor and hid under the table like I'd done when I was a little kid, I would have.

I closed my eyes for a long second. Opened them. Met Bowers' straight on.

"Seth Collins."

FOURTEEN
NICOLE
DECEMBER 23, 1991

I could see that it took almighty effort for Bowers to not gasp. For a man who'd seen it all, I'd managed to surprise him.

Great.

I wasn't going to get anything for the shock value of my originality.

"That same pastor who's on TV? Not another Seth Collins?"

I could desperately see he wanted it not to be true. He wasn't ready to be separated from his illusions. Mine had been shattered. His should follow.

"One in the same."

"I'm sorry. I uh...didn't realize."

"It's okay," I said, but I had to wonder how I'd become the one doing the consoling.

"He's a handsome guy. If he weren't in the church, he'd probably be on the other magazine's cover as the

Sexiest Man of the Year. A lot of girls were lining up to date him a few years back. Rosalee was lucky to get him."

God's Right Hand beat Sexiest Man of the Year any day.

"Why are you telling me this?" I asked, my voice getting hoarse as I tried to hold back tears. "I never wanted to date him."

"You're not the first to come in here confused about something that happened with him. Everyone in Baton Rouge knows that women throw themselves at his feet every damned day. Some do it with casseroles. Others with clothes too tight for church."

"I did not throw myself at him. Are you interested in hearing what happened or should I just get my daddy to carry me back home?"

"I'm a bit surprised your daddy brought you in here," Bowers said.

Reluctantly, the detective extracted a pen from his breast pocket and clicked it so the ball point was extending from the tip. He pulled a pad back toward him. I hadn't really noticed that he'd pushed it to the far side of the table once I'd named my attacker.

"Give me your story from beginning to end."

So I did. I told him how my father had arranged for the interview in New Day's Media relations department. About Collins offering me the job on the spot. How Seth had become my self-proclaimed mentor. I told Bowers all that before I got to the night of Thanksgiving. My own voice sounded robotic to my ears as I talked about the things Seth Collins had taken from me.

My dignity.

My sense of safety.

My respect.

My sexual autonomy.

My right to say no.

"Did you go to the hospital?"

I nodded emphatically.

"For my foot." It was easier to describe the pain the glass had inflicted than the humiliation Seth had caused.

"What about the other? Did you get the"—he waved his left hand uselessly—"exam?"

Even without him saying, I knew what kind of exam he was talking about.

"I did. The hospital in Metairie is holding everything."

I avoided that word, the one everyone on the sexual assault team had used: evidence.

My body was the evidence I never wanted anyone to see.

"If you make a complaint, we'll be sure to collect everything." Bowers was shifting in his own seat.

"If?"

"I'm going to give it to you straight, Nicole...Ms. Long. This is a hard road that you're thinking of going down. I suspect your father has more to do with you being here than you do. It's not a path to take unless you're fully committed. You understand?"

"Tell me." I suspected he'd seen my kind of situation more than once. Angry fathers yanking their daughters down to get the law to punish boys and men for defilement. It was common enough to have become a cliché.

"This...what you did here...and maybe at the hospital or to your mom—"

That last word jolted me. For a stretch I didn't hear a word coming from the detective's mouth, though it was moving. The last weeks had almost been too much.

I didn't know when I was going to talk to the woman I'd thought was my mom or the woman who was my mom. But I needed to have those talks. I didn't think I'd be able to live with the uncertainty of not understanding how the very fact of the origin of my existence could be altered so easily.

"—again and again," Bowers was saying.

"That doesn't seem hard," I said. Seemed like the right answer to all the objections he was throwing my way.

"That's the hard part for some. For others it will be the defense attorney digging into your background."

"Is that allowed?" Seth Collins may have been a sinner, but I hadn't been a saint. "How can anything I did in the past matter?"

"It shouldn't but it does. You'll need to think long and hard about how many men you've had relations with. When you started doing that with boys. If you had any kind of reputation...that may come back to haunt you."

"He raped me. He used his key. Came into my apartment. Forced me down on the bed and took what I wouldn't give him."

"Had you been drinking?"

"It was Thanksgiving. I'd had some wine at home. Then I had poured myself a nightcap. I gave him a glass of the same bourbon I was drinking."

"When both people have been drinking, their perceptions can be altered."

"What does that mean? That his had been altered to think I was willing?"

"When people drink, their inhibitions are lowered. It's why women and men go to bars."

"I wasn't at a bar. I was home and, I thought, safe."

"There's also the aspect of your job. There's a safe bet some will think that you did it to get ahead."

Mentally I took note of Bowers' implications. Either I was a slut, or I was trying to sleep my way to the top. Or both. The inferences weren't pretty. No matter what happened I wouldn't be able to stay here in Louisiana. I could see that now as plain as day. But before I left, I think I needed to see justice be done.

"Do you think a jury will believe me over him? Do you think he'll go to jail?"

"This is not a stranger rape where a big black guy pulled you into a dark New Orleans alley during Mardi Gras. This is someone who knew you. A respectable guy with not only a beautiful wife, young children, but also a church and a pulpit."

His example jarred me. Is this what my life would be like going forward? Every time someone said something about black people, I'd feel some kind of sting of pain or jolt of responsibility to change their mind. Would I have to change this detective's mind about Seth Collins? That was a lot of persuasion I wasn't trained for. Suddenly I felt as defeated as I had the night it had all happened. My foot, which had been healing, throbbed in a kind of sympathy.

"I'll tell you what I'm going to do." Bowers fished in his pocket a second time. "Here's my card. I want you to take a week or so.... Enjoy the holidays. Spend time with your family. Then I want you to call me after New Year's Day and let me know if you want to proceed. If you say yes, then I'll take it from there."

I took the card, palmed it. Right then, I knew I'd never use it. The cost was going to be too high.

FIFTEEN
NICOLE
JANUARY 3, 1992

'm ready," I had said to Daddy an hour ago. We'd just pulled into the Baton Rouge Police Department's circular drive a second time. I tried to swallow past the dread. The moment I stepped foot onto the rape unit's floor, it would all be downhill. I was gearing up for the trip to the bottom.

This was the first time I'd been back to Baton Rouge after the meeting with the police detective. No one from New Day had called or asked where I'd gone. At some point, Daddy or Aubrey's husband must have picked up my stuff, because it appeared one day in the guest room where I was sleeping again. Mam had stopped pulling the bolt-of-fabric-on-the-bed trick. My favorite foods appeared at every meal. Everyone was treating me with kid gloves. Even Aubrey.

Neil Bowers was waiting for us at my appointed time. He took us up to his floor. This time Daddy and I were in the conference room together. I tried not to shift uncomfortably in my chair. Once we each had a cup of water in front of us, Bowers closed the door and took a seat opposite.

Prepared this time, he held a file in front of him. He slapped it down on the table with more force than necessary.

"Nicole, I'm glad you could come. I understand that you're ready to file charges?"

My nod was just a ducking of my head.

"Before we start this process, there's something I want to discuss with you."

I titled my head, curious. When I didn't speak, Bowers cleared his throat.

"A file has come across my desk, and I need to review the contents with you."

"Oh...okay," I murmured as I tried to imagine what kind of thing would come across his desk. Maybe there'd been some mix-up with the rape exam at the hospital. Panic filled me. Maybe the blood tests pointed to my real mother. That wouldn't make sense, though.

Who my mother was or wasn't had no bearing on what Seth Collins had done to me. I must have tuned out for too long because the next thing I heard was my name as a question from Bowers' lips.

"Sorry. What were you asking?"

"If you were sure the...relations between you and Seth weren't consensual."

I looked at daddy. He looked away. Couldn't meet my eyes.

"Consensual? He's like forty. I answered your questions before. He came into my apartment uninvited. He pulled me naked from the bathtub. This wasn't a date gone wrong. This was my boss taking advantage of me. He used a key. I thought I'd locked him out." I stopped speaking when tears clogged my throat.

"I'm a thorough investigator," Bowers said, appearing unmoved by my explanations. "After our first meeting, I drove over to New Day to interview him. Get his side of the story."

"His side?"

"As a defendant, once he's charged, he has the absolute right to defend himself within the bounds of the law. That includes the option to testify in open court as to his perception of what occurred Thanksgiving night."

"He...I didn't say yes. I didn't want that. I didn't consent." Though I spoke the absolute truth, my protest sounded weak.

"How much alcohol do you think you had that night?"

I glanced at my father. Not that I would have lied, but I'd have maybe minimized it to some degree. Then I thought again about the blood test. Had the hospital tested my blood alcohol level? I had no idea what numbers would make me drunk versus those that would make me sober.

"There was wine at dinner. I'm not sure how much I had." That was the truth. My dad was a heavy pour, though. He never let anyone's glass stay empty of alcohol for too long.

"One glass. Three?"

"Probably closer to two," I hedged. "I didn't drink in

the last hour or so because I knew I'd have to drive to Baton Rouge. Seth had left a message with Daddy that I needed to come back."

"Did you feel intoxicated when you got to your apartment?"

"No, just tired. It was raining and I had to watch myself on the road."

"You had a drink once you were back in your apartment?"

"It had been a long day with my niece and nephew running around screaming," I said with all the diplomacy I could muster. I didn't look at Daddy then. He loved his grandchildren, even though their voices were always in screech range. "I keep some bourbon there. Maker's Mark."

"That has a kick?"

"Ninety hundred proof," I admitted. Daddy had always told me that anything less wasn't worth the time it took to pour.

"How much?"

"A finger, I think. I may have added a little more after Seth got there, when I poured the drink he asked for."

"Who's Christopher Sullivan?"

My heart nearly leapt out of my chest at the mention of my ex's name. Whenever I thought I was over that breakup, someone would say his name and I'd get all the dreaded feelings again. Love. Hate. Anger. Shame.

"He was my boyfriend when I was in school in Massachusetts," I said. "We broke up before the end of school. He's a financial analyst now." I stopped talking abruptly before I gave more unnecessary information. Had this detective called Chris? To ask what?

"Noah Salazar?"

My mind went wild with worry. I'd had what I would consider a normal life for a woman my age. Of course, I'd never shared a damned thing with my father. Who would? I was an adult, and as far as I was concerned, my sex life was private. At least until this very moment when Bowers was combing through my past like someone hunting for head lice.

If his list were thorough, there would be the names of seven different men—and one woman—besides Christopher. Okay, more like seventeen. I'd had a few...ten...wild moments in the last few months where alcohol had robbed me of my better judgment, though I had zero regrets...well, until now.

"He was a...friend...from UMass. I met him at a party."

"Derrick Wells?"

"Same."

"Gabriel Myers?"

"He went to Hampshire."

"Felix Buchanan."

"We both interned for the CBT network."

"Jim Neal."

"Same. He was an intern as well."

"Greg Osborne."

"We went to Country Day together."

"James Gordon."

"Same."

"What is this?" my father demanded. I wanted to tell

him his objection was like five guys too late. "Who are all these people? Greg was Nicole's prom date."

"Elisa Gomes?"

I could feel my face flush hot. I lifted the water, finished it in two swallows.

"She was at Mount Holyoke with me," I stumbled out.

I was waiting for my father's protest, it wasn't forthcoming. For the last week and a half I was convinced that daddy was on my side. That he was cutting ties with the church, that he was going to help me take Seth Collins down and if New Day fell with the associate pastor, then so be it.

"What's going on here?" I asked the question my father didn't.

"This here...it came from Collins' investigator," Bowers said so matter-of-factly that I had to wonder if this had all happened before. It was like I'd walked on state to a play that had been scripted in my absence.

"What in the hell was *he* investigating?" I banged the table in protest. Daddy still didn't look my way. My head started inching down as I investigated the table's fake grain.

"Your past. Those were some of the people you've been reported to have...consorted with."

Even with my head down, I could feel my father's appraising eyes roam over me. Something I'd never felt embarrassed about, my sex life, suddenly filled me with shame. I'd thought keeping my body count under twenty had been something to be proud of. Bowers and Collins had sullied those otherwise good memories.

Anger ripped through me, and I lifted my head, stared right into Bowers' eyes.

"What about rape shield laws?" I asked. Going to a women's college and taking a couple of women's studies classes gave me a better than average knowledge of feminist issues. Governments weren't great at keeping up with civil rights, but most states at least had laws that prohibited a rape victim's past from being trotted out in court.

Before that sea change, hundreds if not thousands of victims hadn't received justice when a jury decided she wasn't chaste enough to be a true victim. I looked at the back of my pale hand, recalling that I'd learned that black women had been on the receiving end of assumptions of impurity.

SIXTEEN
NICOLE
JANUARY 3, 1992

"Those laws are in place to protect victims." Bowers' answer had been so matter-of-fact that I'd nearly missed the meaning of his words.

"Are you saying I'm not a victim? That a man who used a pass key to come into my apartment uninvited and didn't take no for an answer isn't in trouble for what he did? He violated me. He violated Louisiana law."

"You may well be a victim, Ms. Long. But a case against such a high-profile defendant would subject a woman like you to two trials. One in the court and one in the court of public opinion. Mr. Collins has a reputation to protect, and he'll go all out to do so."

"Is that what he told you during your *interview?*"

"I want you to have all the facts before you make a decision," he said, ignoring the fact that I'd come here because I had already made a decision.

I'd worked in New Day's PR department. I knew

exactly the kind of access Collins had to the press. *Politic*'s American of the year, cable news' face of modern Christianity, the filler of a five-thousand-person sanctuary.

He was the right hand of God and I was a Jezebel there to tempt him. He'd turn his "indiscretion" into the biggest public relations coup ever. He'd cry. His wife would cry. Mascara would run. She and her cherubic-faced children would stand by him.

I'd be the bastard child of an oil man turned pastor trying to bring down the second coming of Jesus Christ.

Wilted. Defeated. I stood and walked out of the room. A few minutes later, Daddy followed me. We stood in the hall for a long time surrounded by ringing phones and clacking keyboards. Without a word, he wrapped a hand around my upper arm. Before I could piece together his intention, he was frog-marching me out of the automatic doors and back into his Cadillac.

"I don't think police and court thing is a good idea anymore," Daddy said with his right hand fisted around the gearshift once we were in the vehicle, its automatic locks engaged.

I didn't speak because I already knew any decisions were no longer mine.

Daddy jerked the car from park to drive.

"This needs to be settled man to man."

His foot punched the gas so hard I could smell the rubber of the tires left on the pavement behind us.

"Where are we going?" I asked though I suspected I already knew the answer.

"To talk to Seth Collins."

Talking wasn't my father's strong suit. My heart sped up when the likely meaning of his words came through.

"Are you going to shoot him? Daddy?" His nonresponse scared me. "Don't shoot him!"

I was no stranger to firearms. I can't remember a time that Daddy wasn't taking me or Michelle to the backyard to shoot cans from the fence, and later to the range. He was a master of the tight grouping.

"If I were going to do that, I wouldn't have you in the car. It would be another Ken McElroy. I'd take him out to the woods and no one would ever see him again."

The way he said it made me think he wasn't kidding.

"Then what?" I asked while gripping the "oh shit" handle above my window.

"Talk."

We sped through the night, weaving in and out of cars that still had Rudolph noses on their grills.

If I was eating these days, I'd have thrown up. Between my dad's crazy, erratic driving and thoughts about what could happen, I wanted to be anywhere but where we stopped: in front of the house Collins shared with his wife and kids who were clueless about what was to befall them.

There was still a life-sized manger out front, a huge Christmas tree the church members had held a lighting ceremony for, and little white twinkling lights everywhere. It was bucolic, everyone's fantasy of a church pastor and loving family man's holiday decorations.

My father didn't bother with the driveway; he skidded right onto the Collinses' lush lawn. That was going to leave a mark that would have tongues wagging by Sunday. Something told me I would never be back in the sanctuary of New Day to see any of that.

Daddy yanked open the passenger door and had his hand on my upper arm again. I'd barely gotten a chance to unbuckle myself before he'd hauled me out.

"You're hurting me," I said. My plea fell on deaf ears. Once again, he frog-marched me to a different door. Daddy only let me go so that his fist could pound on the red painted wood. The unseen brass fittings on the other side of the door rattled in response.

When no one answered, Daddy pounded again, harder this time.

"Coming!" It was a woman's voice. I recognized Seth's wife before she opened the door, toddler on her hip. If I didn't know her personally, Rosalee Collins would have been interchangeable with my own sister. Blond, petite, eternally endearing face. Not quite beauty pageant material, but doll cute. I'd never been that.

"Can I help you?" She tilted her head at my father in faint recognition. Then she focused on me. "Nicole? Seth didn't mention you were coming by. Is there an emer—"

"I need to speak with your husband," my father interrupted.

"Seth's in the family room," Rosalee said. "The Mavericks are playing the Pistons."

I had no idea if my dad had been in the house before or if he was following the sound of the television, but in less than a minute we were in a room with a huge projection TV. Collins was yelling about a referee's call on a foul. The score was fifty to forty-nine. The winner wasn't a forgone conclusion.

"You got a kid in here?" my father bellowed.

Collins jumped from the leather recliner he'd been occupying. Always shrewd at assessing situations, my boss looked from my father to me. I could see the dawning of understanding on his face. He backed toward his desk.

"Stay right where you are!" my father ordered. "You have some explaining to do."

Collins changed tack and rushed to slam the family room door before my father could object.

"Are you here about my indiscretion?" Collins was smooth, I had to give him that. My face had already been hot the moment we'd stormed through the door and was getting hotter by the moment.

"Is that what you're calling it? My daughter said that you forced her."

"We'd both had a little too much to drink." Collins turned his pastoral counseling eyes toward me. He flung his arms wide, stretching his pristine white polo across his chest. "Nicole, if you took it in the wrong way, I'm so sorry. I've been repenting to God ever since that night. Stepping out on my wife is the worst thing I've ever done."

"Stepping out? If there was a tree in here, I'd string you up," my father raged. I hoped Rosalee couldn't hear a thing. That her kids' squeals of laughter were drowning out my life's most humiliating moment. My father's fist had unfurled, and an angry finger jabbed at the air in front of Collins. "You took advantage of my daughter. We're on our way to the Baton Rouge police department right now. I just wanted to give you fair warning."

Collins picked up the remote control. The game went mute. I didn't warrant complete abandonment of the NBA. He smiled his pulpit smile again and spread his arms even wider.

"That's not necessary. No one will come out good from involving the authorities. We'd be forced to expose Nicole's entire sexual history, and that kind of thing can ruin a woman. Even one like her. Maybe even a church."

"The church?"

"You bailed my uncle out of debt when you took over. In order to get you paid back, we need the coffers filled every Sunday. As God's Right Hand, I can go anywhere. Would be welcomed everywhere."

Everyone had a secret. My father had the most, I was learning. I knew he loved me, but he may love money as equally. He wouldn't chance my mother's ruin.

Collins went behind the desk. Opened a drawer. I was still a little bit afraid a firearm would emerge. Despite Bowers' proclamations and Daddy's rush to leave the police station, I still thought Collins had more to lose than me.

A rape charge on the front page of the *Advocate* would tilt sentiment against New Day. The American of the Year would not be enough to tilt the scales back. A little bit of gumption came back to me. I was an adult and I could make any decision that I wanted. Once this showdown ended, I'd go back to the police department. I didn't think

I'd ever be able to look myself in the mirror if I didn't stand up for myself.

Instead of a gun, Collins thumped a manila folder on the desk. A tiny wave of relief rolled through me. It wasn't going to be the O.K. Corral.

"Neil Bowers did give us a primer on rape shield laws," Daddy said, but even I could hear the bravado leaving his voice.

"Then you already know about the background check." Collins waved the folder. His voice was preternaturally calm. "We have some strict moral codes here at New Day. I have to make sure that each and every person associated with the church is upstanding and in line with what we preach."

My father took the bait, flipped through the ten or so pages there. Then he slammed the file closed, plunked it on the desk. Paced back and forth in front of the TV. It was men in uniforms, then my dad. Men shooting the basketball, then my dad. A commercial for beer, then my dad. By the time burgers were on offer, my dad turned to Collins.

"Let's talk terms," Daddy offered. He looked between Collins and me. "Looks like you both have something to lose."

Terms? My father wasn't a cop or a prosecutor or a judge, so any terms he proposed could not include jail. Which in my eyes was the most fitting punishment for the crime.

"New Day can do severance and a promised good reference," Collins offered.

So much for my job. Not that I wanted to keep it. But this wasn't how I was planning to leave it.

"All that plus a payout," Daddy added. "My daughter is going to have to find a new job and I'm not supporting her because of your bad behavior."

"Fifty thousand," Collins threw out.

"Five hundred," Daddy countered.

"She wasn't a virgin and she wasn't that good. One hundred."

I swallowed down the bile rising.

"Two fifty or we're turning right around and heading out to police headquarters." The way my father's voice faltered, I knew he wasn't going to do that. Face potential financial ruin. It was bravado talking.

"Done. Check will be cut as soon as this is papered with a nondisclosure agreement."

"Deal."

Then they shook hands. Actually *shook* hands. I wondered if this was what it was like with slaves on the auction block. Humanity reduced to dollars.

SEVENTEEN

NICOLE

"I knew this day was coming." Aubrey's voice was more world weary than her nearly forty-year-old life would have indicated.

Even though I'd knocked at the door of their small cottage, I had come in before she or Fabien had invited me. Their tiny kitchen was sunny and inviting despite the close quarters. They'd been sitting and eating beignets and sipping coffee. When he saw my face, Fabien nodded in silent greeting, then took his drink and pastry and excused himself.

"Want a beignet?"

I nodded. Aubrey's had always been my favorite. The ones they peddled to tourists in New Orleans had always been doused in too much powdered sugar for my taste.

She placed one before me with café au lait. Mam hadn't let me drink coffee until I was twelve or thirteen, but when her back was turned, Aubrey had given me very milky coffee. It was only one of the hundreds of secrets we'd shared.

"I thought we shared everything, Bree," I said. My voice was petulant even though I knew she'd been an adult and I'd been a child. The secrets had mostly gone one way. She'd kept my secrets. Maybe she'd been such an expert because she was already keeping her own.

"I always knew this day was coming. Twenty-two years and seven months is how long I've waited for the other shoe to drop."

"For nothing is hidden that will not be made manifest, nor is anything secret that will not be known and come to light."

"What verse is that?"

"Luke eight seventeen."

"You always had a near photographic memory. My mama did too. You're like her in a lot of ways."

"Why?" It was a one-word question that held a thousand. Over the last week plus I'd silently contemplated all those other whys and hows and whats and wheres and whens. One lie begets so many others.

Bree didn't answer the question. Instead, she asked another.

"What's going to happen to that pastor?"

Tears welled up, and I batted them away as fast as I could. I hadn't majored in women's studies and even without all those classes, I knew that the history of the world was men doing whatever they wanted with impunity.

"Nothing."

"Nothing?"

"I got severance, a good reference, and enough money to get started somewhere else." I left out daddy's obligation, his complicity.

"Somewhere else?"

"Louisiana's lost its appeal. I was going to move to New York or Boston anyway. I'll just accelerate my plans, I guess."

"Are you okay with that?"

"Remember my wild period?"

Aubrey's nod was swift. I'd confided all that to her when it had happened. She's the one who'd reassured me that I wasn't bad, even though I'd sinned for sure. She's always had a huge well of compassion for human behavior. Now I knew why.

"They all threatened to bludgeon me over the head with it. Whether it was bad press or whispers. In a fight between Pastor Seth Collins and me, there was no way I could win."

"I'm sorry."

"I'll be far more careful in the future. That's all I can do."

"I thought it would be the best thing I could do for you," Aubrey said, finally answering my big question.

I shook my head like a dog with a bug in its ear.

"Growing up without my mother? You thought that was best?" I didn't have to say more. She'd had a front-row seat to Mam's treatment. To Michelle's.

"I was always here."

"Best how?"

"You'd have money and status. The best of everything. You rode horses. Learned piano. Went to expensive summer camps. Private day school all the way through. That fancy college up north."

All that Daddy had bought with oil money. He could just as easily have paid for that while my bedroom could have been a few hundred feet from where it had been. I looked her in the eye and knew that money wasn't the reason.

"What did you mean by status?" I asked, though before the words left my mouth, I knew the answer.

"You'd pass for white. Even with all the money in the world, there's nothing I could have done to give you all the privilege that carries."

I looked at the back of my hand holding the remains of the pastry. It was pale, lighter than Aubrey's, but not much. The thin veneer of Cajun French history laid over the ugly sins of slavery. Gave lots of men in our state plausible deniability that didn't exist in places like Mississippi or Alabama.

"Are you related to Mam?" Her maiden name was the same as Aubrey's. French surnames were as common as June bugs, though.

"Probably same great-grandfather." The 'probably' was there for show.

"Did you ever want to leave here? Work somewhere else?" I asked. Most families like ours didn't have the same setup we did. Like the upstairs/downstairs thing had changed in England after the First World War, our servant system had dismantled around the time of the civil rights movement.

"My mother worked here and her mother before that and before that. It's not a great legacy, but it's the one I was born into. When I met Fabien, he wanted to leave here. We talked about going to Michigan. He even had a shot at an engineering job up in Detroit. I had to tell him about you then. Told him why I couldn't leave."

Fabien must love the hell out of her to work for my father. I couldn't imagine love that unconditional. Aubrey had at least been lucky in that one way if none other.

"And Daddy? Did you love him?"

"I thought so when I was sixteen. He came here all bold and brash and Texan. He'd married your mother because it was the right thing to do. The expected thing to do. She was from a well-regarded family. Texas oil wasn't. He got legitimacy, access to country clubs and important people. She got money."

What wasn't a transaction? I asked myself as I thought of all the money that had been deposited in my bank account yesterday.

"What did you get?"

"I was young. I thought he was the love of my life. I thought he'd leave his wife behind and we'd run off and, I don't know, live in some kind of one-room love nest with you sleeping in a dresser drawer. It sounds stupid now, like a bad novel, but in my sixteen-year-old mind back then it was entirely plausible."

"What happened?"

"James' father came down. Margaret's father did the

same. They had a long powwow in the study. When all was said and done, he was recommitting to his marriage and I got to stay in the back house."

"Did Grandad Charles and Grandpa Patrick make the decision about me too?"

Aubrey nodded.

"That was the deal. I was pregnant. My mother was living here. I had nowhere to go. I got kicked out of school when I started showing."

"Kicked out?"

"I was a junior in high school. Girls in trouble were considered a bad influence on the rest of the pure ones."

"I was born in May..."

"Four days after my birthday. I went to the hospital. Handed you over to Margaret that day. Your family arranged the paperwork. I signed it right after I got home from the hospital. That was it. Mama had that stroke right after and I just took over her job."

"How did you do it? You know how hard it is for me when someone just mentions Christopher's name. I thought for months I was going to die. It still hurts to think about the time we were together. Falling in love. Planning our future. It still kills me how easy it was for him to end things."

Bree had a hidden strength I'd never considered.

"I had to be strong. There was nothing else to it. You were the highlight of my life. It had to be enough. I took care of you when they couldn't. I tried to make up for your mother's preference for Michelle."

"You could see that?"

"She tried. I'll give her that. She tried real hard. I didn't nurse you. She gave you formula. Tried to bond. Maybe if I hadn't been here like a specter, it would have worked better."

"I'm glad you were here," I whispered.

She stood at the same time I did, and I hugged her as hard as I could. We were the same height. Her hair was the same color as mine. When I pulled back, I stared openly. I could see all the similarities I'd somehow ignored. Her fingers had the same knobby knuckles as mine. Where my mother and sister were well-endowed, I was shaped more like Aubrey: thin, no hips, no boobs. I had my father's eyes though. Ice blue where hers were some indescribable color between brown and green.

"I don't think I can stay," I said. It was the first time I was acknowledging the truth of the situation.

"I don't think you *should* stay," she confirmed. "Take it from me, it's hard to outlive the past. You deserve a fresh start."

"I have no idea where I'm going to go. I was thinking about law school, though."

"Why?"

"I didn't get justice. Other people should. I want to prosecute men for the crimes they commit. Someone has to hold them accountable."

"I have a cousin in Atlanta, Albertine." After Aubrey said it, her right hand swiftly covered her mouth. She'd breached the invisible class divide with those words. I was finding I didn't care as much as I would have thought.

"Do you think she'd take me in?"

Bree nodded. "You two are a lot alike. Smart. Stubborn. Resilient. It could give you time to do whatever you'd need to do to get ready for school. It's far, but not too. I'd know you were safe."

"Can you call her? Albertine?" I asked, as a plan formulated in my mind.

"Whatever you need. I'll do whatever you need."

Those were the exact words I needed to hear.

EIGHTEEN
NICOLE "THE RIOT" LONG
OCTOBER 10, 1997 (FIVE YEARS AND NINE MONTHS LATER)

'd have gotten a conviction," Tom Brody boasted. He was the very definition of cocky, probably because his uncle was *the* County prosecutor, our big boss.

"Me too," Michael Betancourt announced.

I chanced a look at the only other female in our group of five young prosecutors-in-training, a young Black woman named Valerie Dodds. She gave me the slightest headshake. There were a hundred words in the movement of her head, and I understood every single one.

"Maybe Lori Pope is losing her touch. A shooting star is bound to fall eventually." Dick Foster was the guy responsible for that stellar bit of observation.

The five of us were all there were in this new class of prosecutors. The Cuyahoga County prosecutor's office had been in a hiring freeze for years. Technically, they still weren't hiring, but attrition had opened a few entry-level assistant prosecutor jobs.

How each of us had gotten here was different, but we

were the exceptions to that hiring freeze. Getting a job during a bad legal economy had offered the men in our orientation group a sense of superiority. Except for Brody, I had only the foggiest idea of what political lever had been pressed or favor cashed in for the others.

I was here because my father had made it a mission to extract every favor imaginable from Seth Collins. In any other context, I think what Daddy had done would have been considered blackmail. I made an effort not to think too hard about any of it. I took what was given as my due and tried very hard not to look back at that dark time in my life.

"It wasn't a simple case," I interjected. *Nothing like mine* had gone unspoken. The trial we had shadowed today had been a single count sexual assault case. The whole Seth Collins debacle was a secret papered over with an ironclad nondisclosure agreement. This victim had gotten her day in court.

"It couldn't have been more simple," Brody insisted. "The defendant had sex with that girl without her consent. That's the very definition of rape under the statute."

That word: rape. It was the title of the sexual assault section of the Ohio Revised Code. I tried not to think about it. Tried never to use it.

Every time someone said the simple four-letter word, it hit me like a punch in the gut.

Despite our orientation in Common Pleas observing a felony trial, we'd start in Juvenile court next week. I was hoping for the crimes to be far less gruesome. It would take time for me to work up to handling rape cases. That said, I hated that I agreed with Brody. I'd have put that guy in jail for all of the law's mandated ten-year sentence.

No woman deserved what the defendant had done.

"I need a drink after that verdict," I announced. I needed a drink nearly every night. Sleep had been elusive the last five years. I'd become a fan of Hennessey while in Atlanta. Cognac brought the oblivion of sleep free from nightmares.

I summoned the bartender and ordered a sidecar. The rest of my group followed suit except for Valerie Dodds who never drank. She'd had the most expensive soda habit of anyone I'd ever seen. Pop, as she called it, cost nearly as much as a happy hour drink in downtown Cleveland.

"Did she consent?" Dodds asked, after we'd all taken our drinks to a big table in the back of the Sidebar. It was only my second time in the prosecutor-heavy establishment. The defense bar had their own, the Tipsy Jurist, a few blocks away.

"The jury must have thought so." I shrugged. When we'd all walked into the courtroom during jury selection on Monday, conviction had been a foregone conclusion. We'd all been dead wrong.

"The defendant was a low-level crack dealer," Foster summarized. "His customer can't pay, so she offers sex with a friend in lieu of cash."

"How did the customer know her friend would consent?" I asked. "No one can consent to sex on someone else's behalf. That's why the *friend* was convicted of promoting prostitution."

"They get to the friend's house," Foster continued. "Our crack whore introduces the defendant and the vic. Next thing, she says that the defendant's prowling through the house looking for something to cover his..." a wave of Foster's hand stood in for the word penis "...with. He gets out a sandwich bag, wraps it with a rubber band around his...privates and they have sex."

Once the facts had been laid out by Pope during opening arguments, even I thought it was a slam dunk. Especially with the crack user having taken a plea for drug possession and promoting prostitution, then turning state's evidence against the defendant.

"Maybe Pope could have prepped the vic better," I speculated. "I think she was developmentally delayed." I wouldn't say anymore out loud. Cleveland was a small town. In my month here, I was learning that every wall had ears.

But I did think the victim's IQ was questionably borderline. It was possible that legally she may not have been able to consent. I'd brought it up at a training meeting before trial. Pope had dismissed me out of hand. The defense attorney for sure didn't bring it up. The case would have gone from forcible rape to statutory. The second had no defense.

"Pope probably thought that little detail of the sandwich bag was a winner," Dodds said.

"It wasn't as if the defendant were exactly an upstanding citizen," Betancourt added.

"The jury acquitted anyway," I said. "A slam dunk

never determines anything until the final score has been tallied."

"Unless it's a stranger rape," Brody said, "it's always he said, she said. It's hard to know what happens between two consenting adults."

"The gist of rape is that the victim isn't consenting," I pointed out. He sounded too much like Neil Bowers for my taste. The whole "no means no" thing still hadn't penetrated the patriarchy.

"I think it's way more gray than black and white, Nicole," Tom explained. "All of us went to high school, college, law school. How many situations were there where people were drinking? There was some kind of flirting or attraction between the guy and girl. They go back to someone's place, then next thing, there's an accusation."

I swallowed the entire contents of my glass. Flagged down a server for another that arrived in under two minutes.

"Are you saying you think these cases aren't winnable?" I was asking partially for my future career in the prosecutor's office and partly for the me that had been in a different yet similar situation almost six years earlier. As dissatisfied as I was with the deal my father brokered, an acquittal of Seth Collins would have killed me.

"I think if you want to keep your win record near perfect, then you don't take them to trial." Brody's answer was nothing if not pragmatic, though self-serving.

"Are you saying you don't indict?" I asked.

"Depends on the facts. Those date rape accusations?

Those I probably wouldn't take to the grand jury. The case like the one today? I'd get an indictment but would force a plea. The victim gets justice, the defendant gets punished, and I get one in my win column."

Brody clapped his hands together like he'd just pushed debris into a dustbin.

"You know that none of those are excuses, right?" Two strong drinks had made me bold. Everyone else tiptoed around the boss' nephew.

"None of what?"

"The victim knowing her rapist. The victim inviting him into her apartment. Going to the perpetrator's apartment. Drinking."

Brody shrugged neither in agreement nor disagreement.

"I wouldn't want my sister to do anything that stupid," he answered after a beat.

"Do you have a sister?" I probed. In the short time I'd been in Cleveland, his family's...infamy had been brought to my attention. All the Brodys in power—from prosecutors to judges—had all been men.

"No. But my mom always said that women didn't have to make themselves victims if they didn't want to."

Anger I hadn't seen coming, but must have been building over the last few days, nearly shot steam from my ears and nose like a taunted cartoon bull.

"You've got to be kidding me. It's the nineteen nineties, not the nineteen fifties. When I get to Major Crimes, I'll prosecute every freaking case that comes my way. We live in a culture that excuses every damn thing that men do to women. I'll clean the streets of Cleveland of every single one of these assholes. I'll bring the power of the state down so hard on their heads, they won't know what hit them. In Amos five twenty-four, the Lord said, 'But let justice roll down like waters, and righteousness like an ever-flowing stream.' Furthermore, Proverbs twenty-one fifteen promises that when justice is done, it is a joy to the righteous but terror to evildoers."

"That's The Riot!" Dodds shouted before she clinked glasses with Betancourt and Foster.

"The Riot. The Riot," all three chanted before the bartender gave them the side-eye.

"Settle down," I urged. Though I did have to smile at the nickname they'd made from my middle name. A name I'd come to be proud of over the last few years.

"You're so good the way you can weave in all those Bible verses about law and justice," Dodds acknowledged. I'd done it before when we'd had to prepare mock opening statements and closing arguments. I didn't quite have a photographic memory, but a lot of what I'd studied in college had stuck with me.

"Religion major," I conceded before I stood and walked to the bar to get a refill. Tom Brody followed behind me.

"You were really good in your mock trial practice," Tom complimented me.

"Gladiator drop shot," I ordered. The bartender raised his eyebrows.

"Strong?"

"Anything less than one hundred proof is for sissies," I said in imitation of Daddy.

"One hundred proof? You sure on that?" Brody asked.

I exercised my right to remain silent.

The very good-looking nephew of the prosecutor only nodded when it was clear that I was as serious as cancer and didn't back down.

"What in the hell is that?" Tom asked when the bartender pushed two glasses across the polished wood of the bar.

"A strong Southern drink."

"I was saying," he continued his earlier thought, "I think we might be good together."

"How so?" I asked. I wasn't sure if he was planning our first trial as co-counsel or planning our first date as man and woman. I was open to either but didn't want to put a foot wrong by misjudging his intentions.

"Of this group," Brody hedged, "I think we're the most serious go-getters. I think it's always a good idea to have likeminded friends."

"Is that what you're proposing?" I looked him straight in his brown eyes. "Friendship?"

"Maybe we'll talk about it next week over drinks?"

I scooped up my shot glass filled with Southern Comfort and my beer glass filled with 7-up and orange juice. I took both back to the table. I didn't even sit before I dropped the shot glass into the fizzy orange liquid, then drank down the entire concoction in two swallows.

I was quiet after that. The SoCo did what I needed it to do, quieted the memories in my head. Of Seth Collins coming back into my apartment. Of him tossing me on the bed. Of him spreading my legs and taking what he wanted, what he thought I ought to give him, without my permission.

I'm not sure how many more sidecars I had after my gladiator, but I was further soothed when someone put a few quarters in the jukebox. When Savage Garden's "I Want You" came on, I couldn't help myself. I needed nothing more than to let loose, to move to the music.

We'd been in the bar for a while and it was nearly full. Happy hour was long over and everyone inside was feeling as loose as me.

The beat of the band compelled me to dance but there wasn't space on the floor. I gestured to a group of guys in suits, and next thing I knew, two strong hands from two different men lifted me. In an instant, I was on the corner of the bar. I kicked off my shoes and closed my eyes. Let the music move me. Let the memories of Seth Collins and the feelings of shame slip away with every beat of the drum, with every guitar riff.

I opened my eyes when the lyrics dictated. I waved my hands toward Brody urging him to come a little bit closer. His eyes, which had been so warm before, were now as cold as flint. I followed his gaze from me to the bar's front door.

Lori Pope was standing there, yellow overcoat and matching scarf draped over her arm. At her waist was a hand; I looked up to see who it belonged to. None other than Liam Brody, Tom Brody's uncle, and our boss, the one whose name was on every pleading we would ever sign, *the* County prosecutor.

Someone must have spilled water or whisky or wine,

because I almost lost my footing. It was only Michael Betancourt's swift reflexes that saved me from humiliating myself any more than I was already humiliated.

When I was able to see past the crowd, half of whom didn't know what was going on, to the half that were members of the state bar, I knew then that I'd have a hell of a time living down my performance.

Seth Collins was winning again. My little habit of drinking to forget was kicking me in the teeth. Everything that I'd been using to hold me together left me then. I closed my eyes and melted into Betancourt's arms.

I didn't hear everything that was said. Only Betancourt's voice pierced my drunken haze.

"I'll get her home safely," he promised.

"Someone needs to protect her." I think that voice was Brody's. "I wouldn't want her to be a victim."

"From herself," an unfamiliar voice said. "She needs protecting from herself."

When I sobered up, I might have to admit they were right.

ABOUT THE AUTHOR

Aime Austin is the author of the Casey Cort and Nicole Long Series of legal thrillers. She is also the host of the podcast, *A Time to Thrill*.

When Aime's not writing crime fiction or interviewing brilliant creators for her

podcast, she's in a yoga pose, knitting, or reading. Aime splits her time between Los Angeles and Budapest. Before turning to writing, Aime practiced family and criminal law in Cleveland, Ohio.

To hear about Aime's latest books first, and to be eligible for member only giveaways, sign up for the exclusive Aime Austin Mailing List here: http://ebooks.buzz/aimenews.

Reviews are gold to authors! If you've enjoyed this book, please consider rating it and reviewing it at your favorite retailer or bookish site.

To connect with Aime Austin
www.aimeaustin.com

aime@aimeaustin.com

www.ingramcontent.com/pod-product-compliance
Lightning Source LLC
Chambersburg PA
CBHW020644180626
46816CB00003B/1109